PRAISE FOR

A *NEW YORK TIMES* BESTSELLER
A *SCHOOL LIBRARY JOURNAL* BEST BOOK OF THE YEAR
AN INDIE NEXT PICK

"Emotionally rich and charming."
—*New York Times Book Review*

★ "Readers will undoubtedly see themselves in these pages. . . .
A well-crafted, entertaining call for middle schoolers
to find their voices and remain accountable in shaping
their own social spheres."—*Kirkus* (starred review)

★ "Heartfelt and hopeful, this novel will encourage
young readers to offer their hand in friendship to kids who,
just like them, might be struggling."
—*School Library Journal* (starred review)

★ "*You Go First* is a brilliant follow-up to Entrada Kelly's
Newbery winner, *Hello, Universe,* and challenges
readers to rethink the rules of friendship."
—*Shelf Awareness* (starred review)

★ "Kelly writes with sympathetic gravity of young people who
feel lost in a world where they thought they knew the way."
—*BCCB* (starred review)

"Intricately drawn."—*Horn Book*

"Erin Entrada Kelly brings readers another beautifully written
story of hard-won friendship."—*BookPage*

"This novel speaks to the many kids who find themselves lonely
in the midst of middle school."—*Providence Journal*

YOU
GO
FIRST

ERIN ENTRADA KELLY

YOU GO FIRST

Greenwillow Books
An Imprint of HarperCollins*Publishers*

This book is a work of fiction. References to real people, events, establishments, organizations, or locales are intended only to provide a sense of authenticity, and are used to advance the fictional narrative. All other characters, and all incidents and dialogue, are drawn from the author's imagination and are not to be construed as real.

You Go First

First printed in hardcover by Greenwillow Books in 2018; first paperback publication, 2019.

The text of this book is set in Garamond MT.
Book design by Sylvie Le Floc'h

Library of Congress Cataloging-in-Publication Data

Names: Kelly, Erin Entrada, author.
Title: You go first / by Erin Entrada Kelly.
Description: First edition. | New York : Greenwillow Books, an imprint of HarperCollinsPublishers, [2018] | Summary: Charlotte, twelve, and Ben, eleven, are highly skilled competitors at online Scrabble and that connection helps both as they face family issues and the turmoil of middle school.
Identifiers: LCCN 2017047338 | ISBN 9780062414182 (hardback) | ISBN 9780062414199 (pbk. ed.)
Subjects: | CYAC: Middle schools—Fiction. | Schools—Fiction. | Friendship—Fiction. | Heart—Surgery—Fiction. | Divorce—Fiction. | Bullying—Fiction. | Scrabble (Game)—Fiction. | BISAC: JUVENILE FICTION / Social Issues / Friendship. | JUVENILE FICTION / Social Issues / Bullying. | JUVENILE FICTION / Family / Parents.
Classification: LCC PZ7.1.K45 You 2018 | DDC [Fic]—dc23 LC record available at https://lccn.loc.gov/2017047338

20 21 22 23 PC/LSCH 10 9 8 7 6 5
First paperback edition

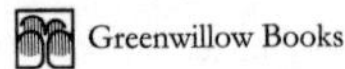
Greenwillow Books

To Marianne

Contents

Part III. WEDNESDAY

Part IV. THURSDAY

Part V. FRIDAY

Part VI. SATURDAY

MONDAY

equilibrium *n* : a state of balance

Girl with a Soda

Rabbit Hole: *Rabbits sometimes dig holes for protection. Once the hole is there, they can crawl inside and hide. Other rabbit holes may lead to vast underground mazes known as warrens, which is where the rabbits live. "Warren" also describes a densely populated building.*

Twelve-year-old Charlotte Lockard balanced an unopened Dr Pepper upright on her hand and thought: *This is what it feels like to hold my dad's heart.*

She'd read online that the heart weighed about twelve ounces.

Same as the Dr Pepper.

She was firmly rooted in the glow of a Crozer Hospital vending machine until a woman with tired eyes and gray hair said, "Excuse me?" Charlotte mumbled a half apology and hurried back to the waiting room, where her mother sniffled into tissues and blamed it on allergies.

Normally her mother wouldn't let her drink Dr Pepper, but these weren't normal times.

Two hours earlier, Charlotte had been in life sciences. A knock landed on Ms. Schneider's door as Charlotte chewed the end of her pencil and stared at the discussion topic on her paper.

There are about 1,500 species of starfish. They live primarily in the intertidal zone, which is also known as the littoral zone or foreshore. Organisms along the intertidal zone are uniquely adept at surviving in harsh environments. Describe some characteristics of the intertidal zone versus the peritidal zone.

■■■

Charlotte had just finished writing "The intertidal zone is the area between the tides—i.e., it exists above water at low tide and below water at high tide—which differs from the peritidal zone, a wider area that extends from above the highest tide level to below the lowest tide level," when Ms. Schneider called her name. Ms. Schneider, tall and lean, stood next to Ms. Khatri, the school counselor, who was short and round. They were opposites side by side. Compare and contrast. And they were both frowning.

"Did something happen to my dad?" Charlotte asked, without getting up from her seat. She felt the other kids' eyes on her. That's when she decided she should probably stand up and follow Ms. Khatri out the door, where she discovered the answer was yes.

He'd had a heart attack and crashed the car in front of Old Navy before being brought to Crozer Hospital for emergency surgery.

And now she was here, drinking forbidden soda and watching her mother read *Us Weekly*, which is something her mother would never read in real life. But Charlotte knew she wasn't really reading it, because her reading glasses were perched on her head. *Eyesight is the first thing to go after fifty,* her mother always said. And Charlotte knew why. The lens of the eye hardened over time and made it difficult to focus—something Charlotte learned after she crawled into a rabbit hole.

That's what her dad called it when she got swept up researching useless information online.

"You've crawled into your rabbit hole again," he would say.

Charlotte sipped her soda. She stared at the WAITING ROOM sign and thought: If you unshuffle and rearrange some of the letters of *waiting room*, you get *migration*, which is kind of the opposite of waiting. It was a good word scramble, all things considered, because her father loved birds. He'd joined a birding club after he retired from teaching art history at Swarthmore College last year. Sometimes he veered off the sidewalk when he walked because he was too busy looking up. If there weren't any birds, he'd look at leaves instead.

"Look at the shape of this one, Charlotte," he would say, a leaf in the center of his palm. "See how the lines branch off here? And see the fringe on the outside? Beautiful, isn't it? Art."

And Charlotte would nod, because she just wanted to get wherever they were going.

Flip, flip, flip. The sound of her mother with the magazine crawled under Charlotte's skin. Charlotte's mother was a statistician and usually hovered over information like a hawk, but she turned the pages so quickly that it was obvious she wasn't reading a word. She just needed to be busy.

"Did you tell Bridget what happened?" her mother asked.

"Yes." Bridget was her best friend. Of course she'd told her.

Charlotte slid down in her chair and stared at a discarded straw on the floor.

“How long until Dad gets out of surgery?” Charlotte asked.

“I don’t know.” Her mother glanced at the clock on the wall. “Soon, I hope.”

Charlotte was prepared for anything. Last year, when her father got a stent in his heart, she went down a rabbit hole and spent two hours watching open-heart surgeries and transplants. She knew what was happening with her dad at this very moment. He was hooked up to a heart-lung bypass machine. They’d probably already stopped his heart so they could operate on it.

Charlotte finished her soda in big gulps and went to the bathroom. Anything to get away from the *flip, flip, flip*.

“Did you wash your hands?” her mother asked, when she got back. “There are a million germs floating around hospitals.”

Charlotte didn’t answer. She secretly rolled her eyes instead. As if she didn’t know about *Acinetobacter baumannii*, a bacteria that teemed on bed rails, supply carts, and floors. As if she didn't know that this species of bacteria could survive for long periods of time and was found in nearly half of all hospital rooms. As if she wasn't aware that it was an opportunistic parasite that preyed on people with weakened immune systems.

"Will we be able to see him when he's in recovery?" Charlotte asked.

"If all goes well. The doctor said you have to be at least twelve to visit recovery and ICU. You lucked out."

Charlotte looked for the straw again, but it wasn't there. Did someone pick it up while she was in the restroom?

She focused on the carpet instead.

"Did you know starfish have hearts, too?" she said. "A human heart can beat a hundred times a minute, but a starfish's heart only beats six times."

Her mother paused. "I didn't know that. About starfish, I mean."

"They're technically called 'sea stars,' but everyone

calls them starfish. We're dissecting one in life sciences soon."

Flip, flip, flip.

The carpet had a hexagon pattern.

The sum of the interior angles of any hexagon was 720 degrees.

Charlotte stared and stared at those interior angles until they barely existed anymore.

Life According to Ben

Part I

Eleven-year-old Benjamin Boxer had played approximately four hundred games of online Scrabble since getting his new phone three months earlier. He'd been dedicated to a single feverish goal: to unseat his nemesis—a twelve-year-old girl named Lottie Lock—and become number one on the leaderboard. He and Lottie had met on an online Scrabble message board specifically sanctioned for elementary school students, but Lottie lost access when she started middle school, so they decided to battle one-on-one to experience direct combat. They only played each other, but their scores were tallied with all the other Scrabble players and thus far, Lottie had nudged him out.

It was a friendly rivalry. They exchanged dozens of texts back and forth over the summer—*you call* that *a play?*, *sorry/not-sorry about your devastating loss*, *prepare to suffer my vernacular wrath*, etc., etc.—but they also complimented worthy performances, like the time Ben played ANT and Lottie won with ANTHEM. So they weren't exactly Superman and Lex Luthor, but still. . . .

Ben considered it healthy to have a nemesis and he was determined to overtake first position with his own username: "Ben Boot," in honor of fellow Ravenclaw Terry Boot, an obscure member of Dumbledore's Army. Then, less than thirty minutes after the end of a school day in September, the unthinkable happened. (Actually, it was totally thinkable, but Ben still hadn't expected it; at least not yet.) Somehow, Lottie Lock had slipped on her game and Ben Boot had advanced to first place with the word VINE, of all things.

Ben immediately took a screenshot and darted out of his room, down the hall, and into the kitchen so he could share the joyous news with his parents, who had—by a stroke of seemingly good fortune—taken the day off. They were certain to lift him on their shoulders and carry him through the neighborhood. In spirit, anyway.

Lucky for him, his mom and dad were already standing side by side, which was kind of weird because they were talking in whispers, and his mom was drinking coffee even though it was three in the afternoon, and their faces were very serious until they heard him come in. That's when their serious faces morphed into something far more concerning: fake nonchalance.

"Ben," his mother said, like he was a long-lost relative who had just appeared for a friendly dinner.

"Son," his dad said.

Things were definitely weird.

"We were just about to call you in," said his mother.

His father nodded. "We have an announcement."

Ben looked from his mother to his father, then sat down at the kitchen island and laid his phone facedown. The joyous news would have to wait, apparently.

The expression on his parents' faces was unfamiliar, so the "announcement" was clearly significant. There was only one thing it could be, in Ben's mind. The three of them were escaping the dregs of Louisiana and moving to Michigan. That's where Mr. and Mrs. Boxer had gone to college and they always talked about going back. Each time the subject came up, Ben imagined himself building snowmen, strutting down the halls of a new school, watching the leaves change color on the trees. Hiking up mountains, even. He was desperate to leave the hot, sticky swamps of south Louisiana and live in the magical wonderland of Ann Arbor, Michigan. He'd never been to Ann Arbor. Or Michigan. But anything was better than Lanester, Louisiana.

Ben sat on his hands so he wouldn't wiggle out of his seat. He was suddenly antsy. The Scrabble victory, coupled with this forthcoming announcement, was too much for his nerves. He packed his imaginary bags, mentally started a new game against Lottie, and inhaled the nonexistent scent of his new school, all while his parents moved even closer together on the other side of the island.

They both started talking at the same time, then stopped. His father cleared his throat.

"You go first, Delia," he said.

Ben's mother looked into her mug and began. "Your father and I . . ."

. . . *have decided it's time to make a move.*

. . . *are finally following through on those Michigan plans.*

. . . *can't live this small-town life any more.*

". . . are getting a divorce."

The room swelled and swallowed him, all while he sat on his hands.

He swayed in his seat. He wasn't sure he'd heard correctly. For one thing, his mother had said it to her coffee, not to him. Plus it didn't make any sense. Other parents got divorced. Not his. Mr. and Mrs. Boxer were

Mr. and Mrs. Boxer. They were both dark haired and gawky. They were both brilliant chemists. They both worked in industrial labs. They were the same age. Went to the same college. They never yelled, fought, or argued, at least not that Ben had ever heard, and Ben was home when he wasn't at school. Ben didn't know much about dating and all that—he knew nothing, actually—but he was certain that his parents weren't the kind of couple who got divorced.

He stuck his index fingers in both ears simultaneously and wiggled them around, like he was clearing the pathways of wax and other obstructions.

"I think I misheard," he said.

He knew he hadn't, of course. But it just didn't make any sense, and he lived in a world of sensible things. Every nonnegative real number had a unique nonnegative square root. *E* was the most-used letter in the English language. Cookie dough was the ideal ice cream flavor. And Delia and Stephen Boxer were not the type of people who got divorced.

"No," his mother said, softly.

She finally looked up, and that's when he knew she was right.

He'd heard it.

Correctly.

"But," said Ben. He didn't have another part to the sentence. Just "but."

"I know it doesn't make much sense to you now," said his father. "But the truth is, relationships evolve over time."

No, no. This was all wrong. "Evolve"? The continued development of a genotype as it interacts with its environment over millions of years—*that's* evolution. Mutations in DNA sequence? Evolution. The differing beaks on finches in the Galapagos Islands: evolution. This was *not* evolution. This was the opposite of evolution.

Wait—what was the opposite of evolution?

Ben's sharp and well-oiled brain became a pile of mush. He couldn't think straight. This was all wrong.

What happened to Ann Arbor? When did this so-called evolution happen? Just last week the three of them watched *Make Me Famous* together. They'd passed objective judgments on the contestants' performances. His father had prepared an enormous bowl of buttered popcorn. Ben remembered thinking: *Look at us, the Boxers, the all-American family, watching reality television together and eating popcorn.*

He'd almost said it out loud, but he hadn't.

Maybe he should have.

Or had they already decided by then?

Surely they had. You don't decide to get divorced in a week—do you?

Both of his parents were looking at him, but they were the ones who were supposed to be speaking—weren't they?

The opposite of evolution. *What was it?*

"Your father is moving into his own apartment, but we're going to stay right here," his mother said. Her hands were still wrapped around the coffee mug.

Her knuckles were white. "We'll still be a family, Ben. We'll just be in different places. And you can talk to your dad or go over to his place any time you want."

Wait—his father had an apartment? When did all this happen?

I should have paid more attention, Ben thought. *I wasn't paying attention.*

"I know it's a lot to process," his father added. "But we'll answer any questions you have. And if there's anything you want to say to us, you can speak freely. You know that."

Speak freely.

Ben opened his mouth, which had become a large, dry, gaping hole with no air going in or out.

"I," Ben said, as if it was a complete sentence.

He tried again: "I."

He looked at his father. He stared at his mother's white knuckles. His heart collapsed on the floor and disappeared into the kitchen tiles.

"I'm first on the leaderboard," he said.

Starfish

Rabbit Hole: *Sea stars' vital organs are located in the arms. If they lose an arm, they have the ability to grow it back. So if they get hurt, they have the potential to grow into something new. Lizards can regenerate, too—in fact, reptiles are some of the world's most resilient animals.*

Charlotte was excited that she was going to dissect a starfish. The impending assignment had taken her down several rabbit holes—starfish led to marine invertebrates; marine invertebrates led to sea anemones; sea anemones led to fossil records—but as she followed her mother to the recovery room, heart thumping with her footsteps, an image sprang into her head and she couldn't shake it out: the starfish, a scalpel, and her hand on both. And then the starfish was gone and it was her father instead.

"Charlotte?" her mother said, once she realized her daughter wasn't at her heels. Mrs. Lockard stopped in the sterile hospital hallway and turned around, both eyebrows raised. Charlotte hadn't realized that she'd stopped walking. Her mother was several feet ahead now, obediently following Dr. Ansari, the surgeon. "Are you okay?"

Charlotte discovered that her voice had disappeared.

She'd told her father about the starfish dissection the week before; how excited she was, and how they'd work on frogs and earthworms later in the year.

"Sounds rather gruesome," he'd said. Not unkindly. Just curious. "You've certainly inherited your mother's left brain."

She had wanted to tell him that the right-brain-versus-left-brain concept was a myth—in actuality, each side of the brain worked together, like a team. Math and science weren't limited only to the left brain, just like creativity and communication weren't only from the right brain. So there weren't really "left-brain people" or "right-brain people." There were just thinking people.

But that would have only proved his point, so she continued talking about starfish and her father eventually got around to talking about seascapes—specifically those painted by Gauguin.

When she was a little girl, he took her to the Philadelphia Museum of Art to show her a Gauguin. She couldn't remember the name of it. Something about grapes. *Grapes in France?* Or something.

"Just wait until you see it, Charlotte," he'd told her, beaming.

At the museum, he stood and stared at the painting like he wanted to become part of it. There were two women in the painting—or was it three? Charlotte stared, too. She thought: *What's the big deal?* She scratched the back of her left leg with her right foot. She leaned on one hip and then the other. She asked if they could go home. When she was upstairs in her room, she wondered if she'd been born into the wrong family.

She used to pretend that she and Bridget could switch places. Bridget loved art, just like Charlotte's dad. She even wanted to be an artist. So Charlotte imagined that Bridget could become a Lockard, and Charlotte could be a MacCauley. She would play with the MacCauleys' dog, Sergeant, and wouldn't have to hear about Gauguin again.

Sounds rather gruesome, he'd said.

And now he was on the other side of the hospital wall.

Recently dissected.

Charlotte's arms erupted in goose bumps.

Mrs. Lockard told Dr. Ansari to wait a moment, then closed the space that Charlotte had created between them.

"Do you want to wait out here?" she asked. "You don't have to go in."

"But . . . ," said Charlotte.

"But what?"

"But what if he asks where I am?"

"He's probably half-asleep," she said. "And if he asks, I'll tell him I asked you to wait outside." She paused. "Okay?"

Charlotte was silent for a moment, then nodded.

When her mother and Dr. Ansari were out of sight, Charlotte still stood there, in the middle of the hall, staring at the door.

Life According to Ben

Part II

The opposite of evolution was devolution. Complex species reverting to simpler forms. It was a contested and controversial concept, but it fit Ben's parents perfectly. They had once been simple, single individuals. Then they got married and became a complex unit. Now they were regressing to their simpler form. No longer a family. Three single units.

Ben stretched across his Ravenclaw comforter. His bedroom door was locked for the first time in—when?

Forever, maybe. His phone rested on his chest.

The first thing he'd wanted to do was call someone. That's what you do when you get bad news, right? You call a friend and they make it better. They tell you that things will be okay. They say, "I've been there, too." But when Ben scrolled through his contacts, he discovered that he only spoke to two people on a regular basis: his parents.

In elementary school, he'd had Adam and Kyle. They weren't his friends exactly, but the three of them sat together at lunch and sometimes talked before and after school. They'd never been to one another's houses or anything, but Adam and Kyle liked to read and didn't mind hearing Ben obsess about Harry Potter or *Lord of the Rings*, even though they all disagreed on various plot points. The worst thing that had happened was the time Ben caught Sherry Bertrand copying off Kyle's spelling paper, and he told Mrs. Havisham. Sherry flunked the test and her parents had to come and pick her up. Yes, Ben felt bad when she was carted off in tears and maybe he was the tattletale the kids—including Kyle—accused him of being, but it wasn't right for Sherry to lift the answers so effortlessly when everyone else in the class worked hard for them. Well, except for Ben. All he needed was to hear a word and he usually knew how to spell it. But still.

Anyway, that seemed like a million years ago. Lanester Elementary was one of several schools that fed into Lanester Middle, and Adam and Kyle had disappeared somewhere in the wide gulf. And they weren't exactly the kind of friends he could call and talk to about his parents' marital devolution.

There was no one except Lottie.

"How pathetic," he said, out loud to the ceiling.

What kind of eleven-year-old didn't have anyone to call with big announcements?

What if he won the lottery? Then what? Who would he call? There wouldn't even be anyone to tell him congratulations. His grandparents lived in the Midwest; he only saw them at Christmas. (And what would Christmas look like now?)

What if he won the Nobel Prize one day or something and wanted to tell someone? Then what?

Devolution. Maybe that was his life: gradually devolving from a boy with two parents and two sort-of friends to a boy with no parents and no friends at all. Maybe he could become a brilliant hermit living off the grid with no modern conveniences except his mind. He'd solve complex mathematical problems in his one-room cabin in the wilds of Ann Arbor (assuming Ann Arbor had wilds). He could get a dog and name it Snape. Or, if it's a girl, Professor McGonagall. And he and Professor McGonagall would have to walk two miles into town just to use the phone and call his parents. *You wouldn't move back to Michigan, so I did it myself,* he would say. Only he'd have to make two long-distance calls now instead of one, and where would he even get the money?

Life was so complicated.

Ben picked up his phone to text Lottie.

Do you think our generation relies too much on digital communication?

Never thought about it. Why?

I was just thinking and it occurred to me that our language has devolved in recent years because we rely too much on digital devices to communicate, like social media and phones and whatnot. I realize neither of us is on social media, having decided it had the potential to eat away at our respective schedules and compromise our academic performance, but we do spend a lot of time on our phones, particularly texting and playing Scrabble and so forth. So I was just thinking maybe we should try to evolve our rivalry, despite the fact that you live in Pennsylvania and I live in Nowheresville. Despite the one-thousand-plus miles between us, we can still communicate verbally rather than relying on our handheld modes of communication. You know?

. . .

Huh?

Um . . .

Do you want to talk on the phone?

ok

Ben sat up in bed, took a deep breath, and dialed Lottie's number before he could think too much about it. If he did, he would have thought: This is the first time I've ever called a girl. Or: I'm talking to a seventh grader that I've never met.

She answered right away.

"Hello?"

"Oh," said Ben. "Hey. It's Ben."

"I figured."

"So . . ." Ben picked at a thread on his comforter. He wondered what his parents were doing. Were they still in the kitchen?

"So."

He wanted to tell her everything. About the announcement. His theories of his parental devolution. Even about becoming a brilliant hermit, and maybe the part about him not having anyone to call when he won the Nobel Prize or the lottery. But now that they were actually on the phone, he discovered that none of those words would come out of his mouth. It seemed like a lot to unload on someone on your very first phone conversation.

"What are you doing?" asked Ben. It sounded like she was in a wide-open space, like a library or something.

"Um . . . nothing. Just sitting, I guess."

"Were you busy?"

"No."

"Me neither."

"So what made you want to talk on the phone?"

"Oh. Well. I kinda had something I wanted to say."

"Really? What?"

He and his parents had gone to the Grand Canyon once, when he was in third or fourth grade. They'd stood side by side and stared into the big, open void, none of them saying anything. It felt like the sky was a million miles wide and they were standing at a cliff in front of it. They'd driven there in his parents' SUV and sang most of the way, until they ran out of songs and settled into their seats to watch the world go by. On the way back, they listened to an audiobook of *Bridge to Terabithia.*

Ben thought of that trip now. It hit him suddenly, like a slap in the face. His eyes watered.

Speak freely, his father had said.

Lottie was silent on the other line. Ben heard something, like an announcement over a PA system. Maybe she was at a train station or something. He wished he was at a train station, because it would mean he was going somewhere. Anywhere.

"I," Ben said, back to one-word sentences.

After a long pause, Lottie said, "Are you still there?"

"Yes." And then it spilled out of his mouth. From where? He didn't know. "I'm running for student council."

He'd passed the posters every day at his new middle school—MAKE A RUN FOR STUDENT COUNCIL! REGISTER TODAY! MAKE A DIFFERENCE!—and each time he thought *hey, maybe I will,* but then he'd forget about it just as quickly. It must have nestled in the edge of his brain somewhere all this time.

"That's great," said Lottie. "Good luck."

"Thanks," Ben replied. "Well. I guess that's it for now. Unless you have any announcements, too? Any big news going on?"

"Um . . ." Lottie was quiet. "I'm dissecting a starfish soon."

"That sounds exciting."

"Yeah. I guess."

"Okay. Well. Talk to you later?"

"Yeah. Talk to you later."

After they hung up, Ben looked at his list of recent calls, and there it was.

Lottie Lock.

"Now I have someone to call when I win the lottery," he said.

Plain and Simple

Rabbit Hole: *Research shows that our brains react differently when we hear the sound of our own name versus other words. There are about 5,163 different first names in common use in the United States. One of them is "Charlotte." About 275,000 people in America are named Charlotte.*

Some people were born to have nicknames. Niko. Mimi. Shonda.

And then there were Elizabeths and Madisons who were never Lizzies or Maddies. That's how the world worked, even if Charlotte didn't understand it.

In elementary school, there was a girl in her class

named Nicole Rodriguez. People started calling her "Nikki," just because. *Do you have a pencil I can borrow, Nikki? Hey, Nikki, can I copy your paper?* It happened organically. That's how nicknames were supposed to work. They crept into the conversation and next thing you know—boom—you had a second name, and only certain people knew what it was.

Nicknames were personal. If you had friends who knew your nickname, it meant you had friends who really knew you. But one day Nikki stood up in the middle of the classroom and yelled, "My name is Nicole! *Nicole!*" Everyone stared at her with their mouths hanging open. Charlotte couldn't believe it. Who gave up a perfectly good nickname?

Charlotte would have loved to have one. Something only her friends called her.

Not that she had a lot of friends.

She just had Bridget.

"Hearing your own name is one of the most powerful sounds in the world," Charlotte's father had once told her. "So you want to make sure people say it the way you prefer."

But Charlotte didn't prefer Charlotte. She preferred something more familiar, like Charlie or Lottie. She wanted someone to lean over and say, *Do you have a pencil I can borrow, Lottie?* Or *Hey, Charlie, can I copy your paper?* But it never happened.

She was Charlotte, plain and simple.

Except when she played Scrabble. Then she was Lottie Lock.

Some people called her best friend "Bridge," but Bridget didn't care either way because she hated her name altogether. She said that "Bridget MacCauley" wasn't sophisticated. They'd tried switching names in the third grade, but in less than twenty-four hours they'd both realized that you can run away from your name as much as you want, but it always catches up to you.

Even Bridget's father had a nickname. People called him "Mac," including Bridget. She said it was more grown-up to call your parents by their first names. She never did it in front of them, though.

"Mac and my mom are driving me bananas," she said now.

Charlotte's mother had taken her home and driven back to the hospital, so Bridget had come over. They walked into the Lockards' backyard on Hampshire Street. Charlotte was glad to have been dropped off, away from the white walls and medicinal smells of Crozer. She was glad, too, that her mother hadn't made her feel like the worst daughter in the world for not going into the room.

"Maybe tomorrow," her mother had said.

Bridget yawned as they made their way across the yard, toward the short stone wall near the pear tree. The wall served as a fence that separated the Lockards' property from their neighbors, the Riveras. Their backyards were side-by-side. It only took a quick hop to perch yourself on top of the wall, which is exactly what Charlotte and Bridget did. They faced each other, like always, with one leg dangled down. They were two opposites together. Compare and contrast. Bridget had thick, auburn hair and perfectly placed freckles that made her look older instead of younger. Charlotte was so spindly that she seemed tall, even though she wasn't. Bridget had curves; Charlotte was all straight lines. Charlotte was wearing last year's sneakers. Bridget bought a new wardrobe at the start of the school year. Charlotte had been surprised at all of Bridget's new clothes, and Bridget had been surprised at Charlotte's old ones.

They were surprising each other a lot lately.

Bridget stretched one of her long delicate arms toward an overhanging branch and snapped a pear from the tree.

"You're going to get me in trouble," said Charlotte. Her mother didn't like when they picked the pears before it was time.

"It's just a pear." Bridget rolled her eyes. "Your mom is so old-fashioned."

That was Bridget's way of saying that Charlotte's mother was old. And she was right—Charlotte's parents were almost the same age as Bridget's grandparents. But that didn't negate the fact that Charlotte would be scolded for Bridget's stolen fruit.

It didn't seem to faze Bridget, though. She tossed the pear in the air and caught it.

"I can't believe your dad had a heart attack," she said. "How come they wouldn't let you see him?"

Charlotte looked down at the stone wall beneath them and cleared her throat. *I was too afraid to go in. I didn't know what to say. Does that make me a terrible person?*

"You have to be thirteen, apparently," said Charlotte. "I can't see him until he's out of ICU."

"When will that be?"

"The doctor said he might be moved tomorrow or four days from now. There's no way to know."

A yellow leaf fell into Charlotte's lap.

See how the stem comes to this triangular point? Beautiful, isn't it? And the color: just like a painting.

But the color wasn't from a painting. It was from a breakdown in chlorophyll. Charlotte knew. Rabbit hole.

"I can't believe your dad had a heart attack," Bridget said again.

"Can we talk about something else?"

"Sure." Bridget tossed the pear. Up, down, up, down. "Tell me about the field trip. How big were Van Gogh's sunflowers?"

"They aren't that big, really."

"I bet the TAG kids didn't even care about them."

On Friday of last week—before the heart attack, when life was somewhat normal—Charlotte had gone on a field trip to the Philadelphia Museum of Art with the Talented and Gifted program—a.k.a. "TAG." Bridget had been furious.

"It's not fair that the TAG students get to do everything and the rest of us dummies have to stay behind," Bridget had said. "Besides, art is my thing. Not your thing."

That was true. Charlotte would have preferred to

go to the Mütter, the medical museum that had bodies and heads and stuff.

"I'll get my dad to take us," Charlotte had offered.

But Bridget had sighed and stomped off. She'd apologized later, but her frustration lingered between them.

"Did you know Van Gogh called the sunflowers a 'symphony of yellow and blue'?" said Bridget now.

"No, I didn't know that."

Bridget turned the pear around and around in her hand.

"Do you wanna play Scrabble?" Charlotte asked.

"No. You'll win. What's the point?" Bridget smiled toward the Riveras' yard and brightened. "Go get your dad's binoculars. Let's spy on Mateo."

Mateo Rivera: the most gorgeous high school sophomore who ever lived. Mateo's younger sister, Magda, was in seventh grade with Bridget and Charlotte at West Middle School but had inherited none of Mateo's mystery. Well, she had mystery, just not the same kind. Locks of dark hair fell over Mateo's eyes, and he always looked like he had a brooding secret that he was dying to tell, if only he could find the right person to confide in. Magda's hair was a perpetual mess. She was one of the top students at West Middle, but she counted to ten with her fingers before every test and tapped on the teacher's desk when she turned in assignments. The kids called her "Mad Magda."

"I don't know where he put them," said Charlotte. This was a small lie. She knew the binoculars were in the drawer under the coffeepot, but it felt wrong to use them while her dad was in the hospital.

"Too bad," said Bridget. She gazed at the Riveras' back door. "Maybe Mateo will come out and you can ask him to play Scrabble."

"Maybe I will." Charlotte smiled. "And maybe I'll ask him to marry me while I'm at it."

"Ooh, little Rivera and Lockard babies! Just think how smart those kids'll be. No one else would ever win anything again."

"You never know. Mateo might not be good at word games."

"I'm sure he is. Look at Mad Magda. Things like that run in the family." She paused and squinted over Charlotte's shoulder. "Oh, God. Speak of the devil."

Magda had just come outside and was walking toward them. She was wearing last year's West Middle School T-shirt, faded and wrinkled; oversized shorts that probably belonged to Mateo; and socks of different lengths.

"Hey," Magda said. She pointed at the pear. "'The pears are not viols . . . They resemble nothing else.'"

Bridget looked at her with both eyebrows raised.

"It's from a poem," Magda said.

"Oh," said Bridget.

Magda turned to Charlotte. "I'm sorry about your dad. Is he okay?"

"Yeah," Charlotte said. She knew the poem: "Study of Two Pears," by Wallace Stevens. She'd written it on a card for her mom's fifty-fifth birthday a few years ago. Her father had given her mother a painting of pears for the dining room—in honor of her beloved pear tree in the backyard—and Charlotte had copied the poem in a card to go with it.

Wind rustled and a shower of leaves fell on them. Bridget immediately brushed them off. Magda raised her arms like she was receiving a gift directly from Mother Nature. Charlotte just sat there. When the breeze passed, Magda picked up one of the fallen leaves and held it gingerly by the stem.

"I can take a picture of this leaf and an app on my phone will tell me what kind of tree it comes from," said Magda.

"Fascinating," Bridget said.

Magda turned to Charlotte and spun the stem in her fingers. "Are you excited about the next TAG trip? I hope it's to the Mütter Museum."

"Uh," said Charlotte. "Yeah."

Magda kicked the stone wall with the toe of her sneaker. "Okay. Well. See you at school, I guess. Tell your dad I hope he feels better."

After she walked across her yard and disappeared back into her house, Bridget shook her head and said, "It's hard to believe a living god like Mateo Rivera is related to Mad Magda. Eggheads are so weird. No offense."

Mad Magda.

Maybe some nicknames weren't so great.

Life According to Ben

Part III

Ben's mother finally knocked on the door at eight-thirty. He was surprised she held out so long. Usually she buzzed over him like a fly. His father had probably told her to give him space, give him time to think, don't smother him so much. He said those kinds of things sometimes.

Maybe that's one of the things they argued about.

Maybe that was one of the reasons.

Ben considered this with each thoughtful knock.

He was still splayed across his bed and staring at the ceiling. He hadn't moved. He needed to pee, but didn't want to leave his bedroom. Things still made sense in here. His comforter. His laptop. His Minecraft universe. The stuffed bookshelves. No one in this room was getting a divorce. Everything was in stasis.

"Ben?" said his mother, her voice muffled. "Are you okay in there?"

"Yes."

"We're worried about you."

Stasis. A state of equilibrium or stoppage. A state of unchanging.

"What are you doing?" his mother asked.

"Playing Scrabble." This was partly true. After he got off the phone with Lottie, he'd started a new game with YEOMAN. But that was more than an hour ago and she hadn't taken her turn yet.

"Do you want to talk about anything?"

"Not particularly."

Pause. "Your father and I feel like we didn't get to have a real dialogue with you about all this. We're sure you have questions."

He had a million.

He had none.

She said something else, and he imagined the words getting stuck in the wood, even though he knew that would never happen because there wasn't enough insulation between the sound waves of her voice and the subpar materials used to build his bedroom door, but nonetheless he chose not to hear and instead thought about what he'd said to Lottie. About student council. School had only been in session for a few weeks, and Ben already found middle school uninspiring. No Adam. No Kyle. He had several different teachers and he didn't mind them too much (not even Mr. Brennamen, who taught advanced history in the most frustrating monotone imaginable), but thus far he had no friends, and now that his parents were getting divorced, it was clear that his entire world was crumbling, one brick at a time, and landing in rubble at his feet. He needed a change for the better. A project over which he wielded complete control.

Perhaps student council was just the thing.

Pear

Rabbit Hole: *Enthusiasts believe that Scrabble is an ideal board game because it's the perfect blend of strategy and luck. You never know which letters you'll get, so there are elements you can't control. But if you know how to use what you're dealt, you can triumph.*

Charlotte's dad was the one who had taught her how to play Scrabble. When she was seven years old, he pulled the game board from the closet and set it on the dining room table. Charlotte was captivated because they never used the dining room table for anything except holiday dinners. It was strictly off-limits—one of Mom's rules—because it was "worth a fortune" and "couldn't get nicked." Later, the painting of pears watched over it.

"Your mom and I played this on our first date," her father had said. He brushed away the dust.

Charlotte's parents had met in the ballroom of the Rosecliff mansion in Newport, Rhode Island. They were on a tour and they were the only ones who "went stag." Charlotte's father, Clayton, secretly worked his way through the small crowd until he was standing next to her mother, Ellen. They looked up at the same time to study the painted ceiling. After the tour, they had lunch and discovered they had a lot in common. They were both in their forties. They'd both gone to Ivy League schools. They both liked to tour historic homes, and they both loved puzzles.

Charlotte's father unfolded the board and shook the bag of tiles under Charlotte's nose—*click-clack, click-clack.*

"You go first," he had said.

She played PEAR, and they both laughed.

After that, they played all the time, just the two of them. The box stayed on the dining room table so it'd be ready when they were.

But last year, the game went back in the closet.

Charlotte wasn't sure what happened, but suddenly there were other things to do. There was too much to worry about. Middle school infected her life like a virus. She started hiding her dolls, even though she still wanted to brush their hair. She slipped stuffed animals under the bed—how babyish they seemed now. And she said no to Scrabble.

That didn't stop her dad from asking.

"How about a game?" he'd say.

"Maybe later," she'd reply.

Eventually he stopped asking. Then the box wasn't on the table anymore.

One day it was there, the next day it wasn't.

When Ms. Khatri told her about her father's heart attack, Charlotte's feet had turned to stone. She couldn't move. For a second she thought she might have a heart attack, too. There was a weight on her chest that wouldn't go away. She had a million thoughts, but the only thing that came out of her mouth was, "I should have played more Scrabble."

T U E S D A Y

gauche *adj* : unsophisticated and socially awkward

Life According to Ben

Part IV

There were two offices at Lanester Middle School. Ben wasn't sure which one did what, so he walked through the door closest to the school entrance. The morning bell would ring in five minutes. He didn't have time to waste.

The office was small and mostly empty, except for a petite blond woman pecking away at a keyboard on the other side of the desk. A bell sat next to a lined sign-in/sign-out sheet. Ben rang it, even though the woman was only a few feet away.

"The tardy bell hasn't rung yet," she said. "You have plenty of time."

Her nameplate said: MRS. D. CARLILE. He wondered what her first name was. She looked like a Diane. Maybe Denise.

An oversized plastic water bottle sat perched next to her keyboard.

"Did you know that the average American uses more than one-hundred-and-sixty disposable water bottles per year, but only recycles thirty-eight of them?" said Ben.

She stopped pecking the keyboard and looked at him. "Are you signing in?"

Ben glanced down at the sign-in sheet. "Signing in? No. I wanted to register for the student council race."

"The deadline was yesterday," said Diane-Maybe-Denise.

Ben tapped his chin thoughtfully. "I wonder if the school would make an exception."

"I wouldn't know. I don't handle the applications. All that's done in the main office." She motioned toward the second office nearby. Ben craned his neck to look through the glass partition that separated them. The other office bustled with activity.

"Which office is this?" he asked.

"Attendance."

Ben looked around. "So what happens here that doesn't happen there?"

"Nonstop action and excitement. A regular carnival."

"Doesn't look too exciting."

"I know. I was being sarcastic." She leaned back in her chair. "The attendance office is where you go when you're late for class."

"I'm never late for class."

"You also come here if you have to leave school early."

"I never leave school early."

"Or if you were absent the day before." Before

Ben could say anything, she lifted her hand. "Let me guess. You're never absent."

"That's right. I've never missed a single day of school in my life."

"If you keep that up you'll get the Perfect Attendance Award at the end of the year."

"Really?"

"Sure as I'm sitting here." She glanced up at the clock. "The bell is going to ring soon. You better get to class."

Ben turned on his heel and headed toward the door.

"Make sure to pick up those registration papers next door," Mrs. Carlile said.

Ben's hand was on the doorknob. "I thought you said it was too late."

"Tell them I said it's okay," she said. "I have a feeling you'd make a good representative."

"Thank you, Mrs. Carlile!" Ben hadn't expected to be so excited. He'd only just decided to run yesterday, after all. And it was completely on a whim. But it felt like something meaningful. Personal *evolution*. "By the way, what's your first name? Is it Diane or Denise?"

"Danielle."

"My name is Ben Boxer," said Ben. "I just started sixth grade."

"Well, Ben Boxer," she said. "Welcome to middle school."

The Anti-Clique

Rabbit Hole: *A winning word at the first National Spelling Bee in 1925 was* gladiolus. *The winning word in 2016 was* gesellschaft, *which refers to social relations based on impersonal ties, such as duty to a society or organization. A gladiolus is a flower that dies in the autumn and winter, only to bloom again.*

The benches in front of the auditorium were prime real estate at West Middle School. Charlotte and Bridget had lucked out: They had lockers within sight of the benches and a well-tuned system that got them there before anyone else. That's where they were sitting when Bridget pulled her hair into a ponytail and said that she hated her art class.

Charlotte thought she must have heard wrong—the hallways were loud and full of shrieks, squeaking sneakers, and slamming lockers, because art was the only class where Bridget finished her assignments. She was a great artist. Like a professional. Before they started middle school, she had talked about art classes nonstop—how they could be taken as an elective and she could take art all three years if she wanted.

"It's because of Tori Baraldi," said Bridget. She sighed and rolled her eyes. Her hair was now in a perfect ponytail. "She keeps coming over and telling me my lines aren't straight or my design isn't big enough or the circumference of whatever isn't in perspective."

"I thought art was supposed to be subjective."

"And what annoys me most," continued Bridget, "is that Mrs. LaPira doesn't do anything. She's, like, this awesome artist, but she never says, 'Tori, go back to your seat, you irritating, conceited gnat.'"

"Why is Tori in art class, anyway?" Charlotte said. "She doesn't seem like the type."

"She calls it her 'meditation hour.' Relaxation time so her brain can rest in preparation for the Bee."

Bridget grinned knowingly and they both burst out laughing.

Here's the thing about Victoria "Tori" Baraldi: Last year, in sixth grade, she made it to the National Spelling Bee. It was a big deal at West Middle School, and for an entire week the students had to listen to Tori spell words over the PA system during morning announcements. There were posters everywhere: "How Do You Spell W-I-N? B-A-R-A-L-D-I!" and "BEE Your Best!"

"Did you know *Victoria Baraldi* scrambles to *diabolic*?" said Charlotte.

"Yes. You've told me that like a million times."

They leaned back on the benches and people-watched. When they were little, they would sit knee-to-knee in the shade of the neighborhood playground and make up stories about all the parents there, like that father is a spy and that mother is in the witness protection program. Mr. Patel was secretly a millionaire with diamonds in his basement. Ms. Gianforcaro's real name was Mrs. White, but she had to flee the country after a bank heist gone wrong. And old Mr. Mruk wasn't old at all—he'd taken a special potion that made him age backward.

When had they stopped playing that game?

It must have been one of the things that disappeared, like Charlotte's thick-haired dolls.

Back then, in elementary school, they were even sort-of friends with kids like Tori and Magda—the "eggheads," as Bridget called them now. Charlotte distinctly remembered holding hands with Bridget and chanting, "Red Rover, Red Rover, let Magda come over."

Charlotte closed her eyes and imagined the smells of the West Elementary School playground. Then she nudged Bridget and tilted her head toward Magda, who was unloading books from her locker to her backpack.

"Hey," Charlotte whispered. "Do you think Magda is in the CIA?"

"What are you talking about?"

Had Bridget forgotten?

"Nothing," Charlotte said.

Bridget eyed Magda and said, "You know how we were joking about you inviting Mateo over for Scrabble?"

Charlotte pictured Mateo at her dining room table, hair falling in his eyes as he pinched a Scrabble tile between his fingers.

"Well," Bridget continued. "That got me thinking. Maybe you could invite Magda over instead."

Charlotte's eyebrows bunched together. "That Mateo thing was a joke. And anyway, that's not exactly an even trade-off," she said.

Bridget laughed nervously. "No, I mean . . . I bet she's really good. You could play after school. She'd be a much better opponent than me, and it would give you something to do until you're able to visit your dad."

"Oh," Charlotte said. "I thought you could just come to my house, or something. Like usual."

"Yeah, but. I mean, she lives right next door to you." Bridget shrugged. "I just thought, since she's part of the egghead clique . . ."

"Well, I'm part of the anti-clique."

That's what Charlotte and Bridget had called themselves last year, because there were only two of them and they didn't have a theme, like "the eggheads" or "the band kids" or whatever. They were just two friends who hung out all the time, even though they didn't have much in common.

After a long pause, Bridget said, "The thing is, I don't think I'm going straight home after school today." She tugged at her ponytail and wrapped a lock of hair around her finger. "Sophie Seong asked me to meet her at Red's . . ."

"Sophie Seong?"

"Yeah. We're in art together this year." Bridget

stood up. "You can come, too, if you want. I'm sure Sophie won't mind. I just figured you wouldn't want to, especially after what happened last time."

Charlotte thought about this science-fiction book she'd read once, where a robot repeated "does not compute, does not compute" until it self-destructed.

"Maybe," she said. But she was really thinking: Me at Red's? Does not compute. Does not compute.

Red's wasn't really Red's. It was JJ's Pizza, and it was just a few blocks away.

Red's was named for the red awning in front. It was an after-school hangout for people like Sophie Seong and her friends. From three to four p.m., the place was packed with "cool" kids. There was always a way to tell the Red's crowd from the rest of the kids at West Middle School, and this year it was their shoes. It was the "in" thing to wear Vans sneakers with long laces.

Charlotte had only been to Red's once—not counting the times she went with her dad on a weekend, when it was just a pizza joint and not a hangout.

It had been at the end of last year. She had gone because Bridget wanted to see what all the fuss was about, but first Bridget wanted to put her hair in a messy bun, because that's what all the Sophie Seongs were doing. So they'd stopped at Charlotte's house to get a rubber band and bobby pins. Her dad was in the kitchen, sorting through his prescriptions.

"Hey there," he said. He was putting pills in little containers marked for the days of the week. *Clink, clink, clink.* "What're you two troublemakers up to?" He smiled at Bridget. "Paint any masterpieces lately?"

Bridget gave her usual reply: "Still working on it, Mr. Lockard."

"Practice makes perfect." That's what he always said.

"Right now I'm trying to sketch things from life, like that." She motioned toward Mrs. Lockard's pear painting in the adjoining dining room. "But it never turns out right. Like, the bowl of fruit doesn't look like a bowl of fruit."

"What does it look like?"

Bridget thought about it. "Worms."

Mr. Lockard laughed. "Maybe you can be the next Van Gogh. If he painted a bowl of fruit, it wouldn't look exactly like the actual bowl. It looked like someone's dream of one. It's remarkable, actually. And there's a Van Gogh at the art museum."

Clink, clink, clink.

Charlotte tugged Bridget's shirt toward the stairs. "Let's do your hair so we can go."

"Where you off to?" Mr. Lockard asked. All the pills were tucked away in the compartments, so he shut the lids. *Snap, snap, snap.*

"Red's," said Charlotte.

"Red's! Now there's a blast from the past." He rubbed his belly. "Pizza sounds delicious. Maybe I'll join you. My treat, of course."

The girls said nothing then hurried up the stairs with matching panic in their eyes. Once Charlotte closed the door, Bridget said what both of them were thinking: "I like your dad and everything, but . . . he can't come. He just can't. It will be mortifying. MOR-TEE-FYE-ING." She paced the room, opening and closing her palm, as if to say gimme-gimme. "Where's Sphinx? *We need Sphinx*."

Sphinx was a piece of quartz from Egypt. One of Mr. Lockard's colleagues at Swarthmore College had given it to Charlotte as a gift, because she wanted to be a geologist one day. She had a collection of more than one hundred rock specimens in trays on her dresser, each with an identifying label—hematite, pegmatite, pyrolusite, feldspar—but the quartz was her favorite. At some point she and Bridget had decided that it brought them good luck and they named it Sphinx.

Sphinx was always in the same place—in the tray, marked Egyptian quartz. Charlotte snatched Sphinx and shoved it in Bridget's hand. Bridget stopped pacing and cradled the quartz to her chest.

"Please, Sphinx, make Charlotte's dad change his

mind." She pushed the quartz toward Charlotte. "Now you."

Charlotte took it but didn't make a wish. Instead, she said, "I'll just tell him not to come." She put Sphinx back in its place.

Bridget exhaled and collapsed on the bed with her back facing Charlotte: her way of saying let's get started on the bun.

"Okay," Bridget said. "What will you say?"

"I'll just tell him the truth. I'm sure he'll understand."

Bridget paused. "Maybe. But your parents are different. They're so . . . old-fashioned."

In elementary school, Bridget had thought Charlotte's parents were an unending trove of interesting stories. Particularly Mr. Lockard, who had been to the Sistine Chapel, could name at least seventy shades of green, and had an old record player where he'd spin David Bowie records.

But that was then.

Ten minutes after wishing on Sphinx, Bridget had a

perfectly imperfect bun on top of her head.

"Do you want one, too?" Bridget had asked, moving locks of her hair without looking at Charlotte. "I mean, it might make us late, but I can do it."

Charlotte's hair suddenly felt unnaturally long and heavy.

"No," Charlotte had said. "I don't want us to be late."

Good thing, because Bridget was already halfway to the stairs.

Maybe my dad changed his mind, Charlotte thought, as her sneakers hit each step. *Maybe he realized how ridiculous he was.*

A parent at Red's after school? It just wasn't done. Even she knew that.

But when Charlotte's foot hit the final step, she saw him sitting in his recliner with his jacket on, the one he always wore even though her mother insisted he needed a new one. He was wearing his Phillies cap and had the house keys in his hand. He stood up when he saw them, and smiled.

"Ready?" he said.

Charlotte and Bridget exchanged looks.

The back of Charlotte's neck felt like it was on fire.

"Um," said Charlotte. She glanced at Bridget, but Bridget looked away this time. "Actually, Dad? We kinda . . . well, we wanted to go by ourselves."

Mr. Lockard's smile faded. He nodded like he'd just been told the solution to a problem he hadn't known existed.

"I mean . . . ," continued Charlotte. "It's just kinda embarrassing, you know?"

"Oh," Mr. Lockard said. "Yeah, of course." He cleared his throat and tapped his forehead. "Senior moment!"

The girls laughed uncomfortably.

"I've got stuff I need to get done around the house, anyway." He pulled his wallet out of his back pocket and gave Charlotte a twenty, which was enough for two visits to Red's. "Dedicate a slice to me."

Life According to Ben

Part V

Ben entered the lunchroom like George Washington crossing the Delaware. It was the evolution of Ben, day one. Time to meet people. He was already so far behind. In the campaign. In adolescence. In life. He didn't even know who his opponents were, but it didn't matter. He would run on his own merits.

He straightened his shoulders and stood tall. He cleared his throat and wiped his sweaty palms against his pants. His heart thundered, but if he wanted to win this battle, he had to charge through his fears.

His shoes *click-clacked* as he made his way through the double doors, but no one noticed him. The lunchroom was noisy, much noisier than the one at Lanester Elementary, which he hadn't thought possible. Recyclable materials were everywhere. Crinkling water bottles. Dented soda cans. Plastic straws. The rectangular tables overflowed with them. They also overflowed with sixth graders. There were boys to his right, hunched over an iPad. There were girls to his left, popping sodas open. Kids were everywhere—pushing out and pulling in chairs, balancing lunch trays, biting apples, shoving food into their mouths, talking and gawking and losing themselves in conversation.

Ben eyed them, wondering who he should approach first.

He decided on the iPad table.

The boys were huddled around a game he didn't recognize. Something with zombies strutting out from wrecked cars. A boy in a Louisiana State University

Tigers hat splattered one of them just as Ben walked up.

"Oooh, Theo, that was awesome," the other boys said, in succession.

Ben had a low opinion of zombies as combatants, so he was less impressed. Not that he was going to say so. Zombies technically didn't have brains, so they would fail miserably in a battle of wits, logistically speaking. If Ben ever encountered a zombie, he'd repeat the famous quote attributed to Shakespeare: "I would challenge you to a battle of wits, but I see that you are unarmed." Not that video games needed logic. Minecraft didn't make much sense either, if you really thought about it. You can't build a waterfall in the middle of an erupting volcano, for example. Not that Ben had ever tried to do that. But still.

"Uh. Who're you?"

Ben blinked. He heard the groans of a dying zombie and nothing else. A hundred pairs of eyes looked back at him. At least it felt like a hundred. Theo and his friends were gaping as Ben stupidly stood there. A burn of embarrassment bloomed in his chest, but he willed it away and stuck out his hand.

"Hi," he said, as cheerfully as possible. Channel your inner President Carter, he told himself. Friendly and personable. Friendly and personable. "My name is Ben Boxer."

They studied Ben's hand like it had sprouted from his nose.

A robotic voice grumbled from the iPad: "Would you like to continue, soldier?"

"I'm running for student-council president," announced Ben.

Theo raised his eyebrows. "And?"

"And I'd love to have your vote!" Easy does it.

The boys waited for him to say something else.

"I've never missed a single day of school," said Ben. Show of dedication.

"And I'm a friend to the environment," he added. Show of personal values.

"Which environment?" said Theo. "Pluto?"

The boys erupted like hyenas, but the joke was on them. Pluto could never sustain complex life forms, much less humans. Pluto's atmosphere sustained winds of up to 225 miles per second, and the temperatures sometimes reached minus 387 degrees Fahrenheit.

Only.

The joke wasn't on them.

Not really.

That much Ben knew.

"Thanks anyway, guys," Ben said.

He pivoted on his heel and approached the neighboring table. Nothing in this world can take the place of persistence. So said Calvin Coolidge.

The next table was full of girls with identical ponytails, right down to the type of ribbon. The only difference was the color of the ribbon and the shade of the ponytail.

Yellow Ribbon was holding court. She had just asked the others if they could change one thing about themselves, what would it be? When they all fell silent to think, Ben said, "Nice ponytails."

They swung his way.

"My name is Ben Boxer." He stuck out his hand.

The girls exchanged looks, unsure of what to do. Finally the one closest to him—Purple Ribbon—shook his hand, and he continued on: "I'm running for student-council president, and I'd love to have your vote."

"Ben Boxer?" Yellow Ribbon said, like it was a dirty word she needed to spit out. She didn't wait for him to answer. She huffed and not-so-casually stifled a laugh with her closed fist. "Yeah, we know."

"We do?" said Purple Ribbon.

There was something familiar about Yellow Ribbon. Ben's mind went through a series of mental flash cards. Yes, he knew this girl from somewhere. But where? It's not like he was acquainted with a million girls. He wasn't exactly Mr. Popular. Clearly. But this experience would change that.

The evolution of Ben.

Day one.

"Yes," the girl said. "As in, Ben Boxer—biggest *dork* in school."

That's when he realized who she was.

Sherry Bertrand.

The girl who had cheated off Kyle's spelling paper that time.

The girl who had been carted off in tears under the shadow of Ben's accusatory finger.

"Uh," said Ben.

"Also," Sherry continued, glaring at him. "That whole running-for-president thing? And wanting our vote? Not. Likely."

"Uh," said Ben.

"News flash. You have to be in eighth grade to run for president. And you are so obviously not in eighth grade. You don't even look like you're in sixth grade. More like third, tops. Sixth graders can only run for treasurer and there's no way you'll win that, either."

"Ouch, Sher," Purple Ribbon said, frowning. "Do you have to be so—"

"Listen," Sherry said, leaning forward on her elbows. "You won't win treasurer because *I'm* running for treasurer. So . . ." She spread her arms, palms up, and shrugged, as if to say: *So there's really no point for you to be in the race.*

"Oh," said Ben.

"Did you know you have to give a speech in front of the whole grade on Friday?" Sherry fake-frowned. "That's a lot of pressure for a third grader."

The girls laughed. Not quite the howls from the boys' table, but a laugh was a laugh when it was at someone else's expense.

"Good one," mumbled Ben, his throat suddenly dry. He half waved and turned, saying, "Nice to meet you" as the laughter carried on.

Not Just Lunch

Rabbit Hole: *In 2017, Haitian immigrant Denis Estimon started a club at his Boca Raton high school called We Dine Together. Its purpose is to make sure no one eats lunch alone.*

Lunch wasn't lunch at West Middle School. Yes, they served food, but most kids got a bag of chips and a soda and sat outside. They all had their own spots, including Charlotte and Bridget. They made their way to the big tree near the soccer field and sat in its shade.

"Hey," Charlotte said, squinting in the sun. "I was thinking—if you wanna hang out with Sophie, maybe . . . I don't know, maybe the three of us could go somewhere. She could come to my house. Look at my dad's art books or something."

Bridget used to love sitting on Charlotte's bedroom floor with one of Mr. Lockard's heavy coffee-table books spread across her lap. She and Charlotte would look at Michelangelo's naked statues and giggle.

"Oh, speaking of Sophie and art books . . . ," said Bridget. "Sophie had an idea to start an art club and she asked me to join. Dee Dee Montgomery will be in it, too. She's in our class."

Charlotte noticed that she said *our* class instead of *my* class, and somersaults turned in her belly.

"We mapped the whole thing out this morning," continued Bridget. She popped a Cheeto in her mouth. She could eat a whole bag without her fingers turning orange. It was the way she held them, with the very tips of her painted fingernails.

When had she started painting her fingernails, anyway?

"Do you want to invite her to my house after school?" asked Charlotte, after a long pause. "Instead of going to Red's, I mean. Maybe some of my dad's books will help with the art club."

"I don't know." Bridget sighed. "I guess I can ask."

"If not, I can help you with your homework, if you still need it. That is, if you don't go to Red's or something. Last week you said you needed help studying for Mr. Groskin's social studies test."

Bridget looked into her bag of Cheetos like she was talking to them. "Yeah, sure," she said. She paused. "So . . . about art club."

Charlotte watched an ant crawl in the dirt in front of them. "Yeah?"

"We'll probably have our meetings over lunch. Because Sophie can't stay after school most days. She has soccer practice."

Somersaults. Tumble, tumble, tumble. They defied

gravity. They somersaulted into Charlotte's throat and turned into a huge knot.

"But Sophie doesn't have A lunch," Charlotte said.

The students at West were divided by A lunch and B lunch. The summer before sixth grade, Bridget and Charlotte had held Sphinx together and wished with all their might that they would get the same lunch.

"Sitting alone at lunch is a fate worse than death!" Bridget had said, her hand clasped over Charlotte's. "Help us, Sphinx!" And even though they meant it, they'd exploded into giggles.

When they both got A lunch, they attributed it to the irrefutable powers of Egyptian quartz.

"I know," Bridget replied. "She has study hall, and she already asked if she could use it for art club meetings."

"But . . ."

Charlotte left the word hanging there and hoped Bridget would latch on to it.

She didn't.

Life According to Ben

Part VI

There is nothing to fear but fear itself. So said Franklin Delano Roosevelt.

Ben had pumped himself up by the time sixth-period advanced English rolled around. He was skilled at it. His father had taught him that half of life was attitude. You may have smarts, his father had said, but if you don't have the right attitude, nothing else matters.

Ben wondered what his father's attitude was toward his mom, now that they were devolving?

What was his father's attitude toward him?

Oh well. That may have mattered yesterday, but it didn't matter now. Today, he had something more important to think about.

Yes, he'd been slightly—okay, more than slightly—defeated in the lunchroom. But success didn't come easy to anyone. Take Darwin's finches in the Galapagos. Their beaks changed with the ecosystem. They didn't just shrug and say, "Oh well, some finch in a baseball cap made fun of my beak, so I'll just go extinct now and forget about survival." The finch straightened its feathers and said, "I will sharpen my beak and change the world of science forever!"

Ben needed to do something bold like that.

Something to go down in the history books.

The courage swelled inside him. Increasing levels of determination fired through his brain as Ms. Abellard stood in front of the smart board, providing literary definitions that he already knew. His knee, trying to contain all the unfettered enthusiasm of a man with a plan, bobbed up and down, and before he could stop himself, he sprang from his seat and stood next to his desk. The movement was so sudden that the chair scraped against the floor and everyone—including Ms. Abellard—turned toward him.

Ben realized he was holding his pencil, so he used it to tap the top of his desk.

"Ms. Abellard, I'd like to make a brief announcement, if I could," he said. He could hardly stand still. He bounced up and down on his toes.

Ms. Abellard raised her eyebrows. She was still pointing to the definition for story arc.

"Do you need to use the restroom?" she asked.

John, Dan, and Eddie—the boys who sat around him—snickered.

"No, ma'am," Ben said. "I just want to make a brief announcement regarding my candidacy for student-council office."

"Oh," Ms. Abellard said. Her eyes darted around the classroom. "Well—"

"It'll only take a moment," Ben said, quickly. "I promise."

Another chair scraped against the floor.

"Ms. Abellard, this is an unfair advantage!" said Sherry Bertrand.

Ugh. How could he have forgotten she was in this class?

Maybe because he never knew in the first place.

Now that he thought about it, he never spent much time noticing any of the other kids. He typically kept his eyes ahead, listening to the lecture, taking notes, disappearing into his mind, which operated with much more finesse than the minds of other eleven-year-olds.

What else had he missed?

"If *Ben Boxer* gets to make a totally random 'speech' to the class, then I should make a speech, too." Sherry crossed her arms and smirked. Ben studied her face. Her lips were pale pink and shiny, and she was dressed like a mannequin at the mall.

Ben cleared his throat and turned to the teacher. "She's right. It's only fair."

Ms. Abellard waved her dry-erase marker in the air. "I don't think this is the place for anyone to—"

Ben turned to Sherry. "You can go first," he said.

Sherry shook her head. Her ponytail flopped from one shoulder to the other. "You go first, Ben Boxer. By all means. Be. My. Guest." She sat down in her chair delicately. The girl in front of her—also dressed like a mall mannequin—leaned over and whispered something, and they giggled. The boy behind her—Derrick Whatshisname—gave her a thumbs-up.

No one was giving Ben a thumbs-up.

No matter.

Ben cleared his throat a second time. "I want to go to work for you." He swept an open hand around the room. You're always supposed to use hand gestures when you speak. He'd read that somewhere. "Each and every one of you." He pointed to specific people—John, Dan, Jeffrey, Laurie, Eddie, even

Derrick Whatshisname. "To do that, you must first elect me to student council." He pointed to himself.

No one had moved a single muscle. Not even Ms. Abellard.

Were they listening, or—?

"I want to know what you think about Lanester Middle School and its student body. I want to hear"—he cupped his ear—"from you." He pointed to the class again. "Thank you."

The room was completely silent. He straightened his desk before he sat down. His classmates stared at him a moment longer before turning back to Ms. Abellard in slow motion.

"Uh," Ms. Abellard said. "Thank you, Ben." She pointed at Sherry with the marker. "Sherry, do you want to . . . say anything? Quickly?"

Now they all turned to Sherry, who grinned.

"On second thought, Ms. Abellard, I think I'll just save the big speech for Friday."

A wave of quiet snickers brushed over the

classroom. Ben's ears thrummed.

They'd been listening—right?

The snickers were for Sherry—weren't they?

You are evolving, Ben Boxer.

You are a finch.

Probably Not

Rabbit Hole: *Earthquakes occur when the earth's tectonic plates reach their maximum amount of stress following gradual friction. A rupture occurs, creating the quake. Earthquakes happen all the time all over the world, but you can't feel all of them.*

Charlotte was in life sciences, staring blankly at Ms. Schneider, and for the first time in days she wasn't thinking about her father. She wasn't imagining tubes coming out of his nose or IVs dangling from his arm. She also wasn't thinking about the scientific theories projected on the whiteboard. She was thinking about a rabbit hole she had climbed into once, when she'd first learned about silent earthquakes.

Scientists called them "slow slips" or "episodic tremors." You can't feel them. There's no rumbling under your feet. Plates don't shatter on the floor.

Red's. Art club. It all felt like a slow slip.

Charlotte told herself: *So what?*

Charlotte thought: *What's the big deal?*

But she was waiting for a rumble. A crash. An explosion.

"Earth to Charlotte Lock-nerd. Wipe up your drool and pass the paper."

That was Tori Baraldi, who sat next to her. She waved a stack of papers in Charlotte's face.

Charlotte took a paper, passed the rest on, and discovered with horror that it was a pop quiz.

1. Give a one-word meaning of "echino-" when used in the following context: A sea star is an echinoderm.

2. Describe the function of the radial nerve in a sea star.

3. What are the functions of the ampulla?

Charlotte chewed her pencil and imagined a different scenario: One where she went to Red's with Bridget and Sophie. She pictured the three of them sitting at a table with plain cheese slices because for some reason girls never ordered toppings at Red's. They were talking about . . . what? Art? Van Gogh? After Mr. Lockard told Bridget about Van Gogh that day—the day he gave them twenty dollars, even though they never dedicated a slice to him—Bridget had started reading about all kinds of "Post-Impressionist stuff." Now she considered herself an expert. That's why she wanted to see the sunflowers at the museum. She said Van Gogh was a "genius." That's probably what she and Sophie talked about in art class. *Oh, Van Gogh! Isn't he a genius?,* Bridget would say. *Ohmygod, you're so right,* Sophie would reply. *Not only that, but Picasso is sooo overrated.*

Charlotte practiced her imaginary response: *Did you know* oasis *is a scramble of* Pablo Picasso? *And* nonteaching *is a scramble of* Vincent van Gogh? *Interesting, right?*

Even in her imagination, their faces were blank.

The day Mr. Lockard told them about Van Gogh was the last time they'd wished on Sphinx. It was the last time they'd gone to Red's. It was the last time Charlotte had heard her father talk about art.

She wrote *prickly* for the first quiz response and took her mind to that day, when she'd said he was embarrassing—even though that wasn't what she meant, not really—and she imagined that instead of going to Red's with Bridget, where they'd sat awkwardly and pretended they belonged there, she'd asked her father more questions. *Why did Van Gogh cut off his ear? Why didn't he just paint things the way they appear? Why did the paintings look like they were in a dream? Was it a mistake, or did he want to paint that way?*

Charlotte knew that all of a starfish's sensory information and memory went to its radial nerve, but her eyes were blurry, and a fat tear fell right where the answer should have been. It soaked through the page. A perfect circle.

Charlotte pressed the heels of her hands against her eyes to push the tears back inside. She sniffled. If anyone asked, she would say she had allergies.

Hey, Charlie, is everything okay?

Yeah, sure. Just allergies.

But no one asked.

Life According to Ben

Part VII

The Boxers' dining room table was covered with white poster board and fat permanent markers, all black. Ben had read somewhere that branding was everything. People recognized the golden arches because McDonald's signs were the same everywhere. It would be the same for him. All his signage would be black letters against a white background. He'd keep the slogan simple, too. Something memorable. BEN BOXER FOR THE PEOPLE. It felt very Huey P. Long, except without the corruption and murder and everything.

There were seven posters, all destined for the sixth-grade hallway. His plan was in place: Make posters tonight, get to school early to hang them, and work on his speech over lunch. He was playing catch-up with Sherry, but no matter. His mind was a well-oiled machine. He would not only conquer student council and Sherry Bertrand, but middle school, adolescence, and then—the world.

"Are you sure you don't want it to be more colorful?" his mother asked. She was hovering again.

"No. Branding. Remember?"

"Ah. Yes."

Mr. Boxer hadn't moved out yet, but he wasn't home, which was unusual for this time of evening. But then again, everything was unusual now.

Maybe he was at his new apartment, wherever that was. *I'll put the new couch here and the flat-screen TV there*, he was saying to one of his new single buddies, whoever they were.

If this was last week, Ben would've asked: "Hey, where's Dad?"

Instead, he let the absence fill the room and strangle all the questions away.

He needed to focus on the posters, anyway.

When he was finished, his head throbbed from the permanent-marker smell and he was hungry because he'd skipped dinner. When his father came home, Ben was standing at the foot of his bed, staring at a selection of clothes to wear the next day. If Sherry Bertrand was going to look like a mall mannequin, he needed to look like something, too. He needed to look like a man with purpose.

"What you up to?" his father asked, knocking on the door and opening it at the same time.

Ben kept his eyes on the clothes. Dark-green dress shirt or white? And which tie should he wear?

"Trying to figure out what to wear tomorrow," said Ben.

His father walked in and stood next to him.

"Getting dressed up, huh? Special occasion?"

Ben shrugged.

"Do you want to talk about anything?" his father asked.

"Not particularly. Unless you have an opinion on whether I should wear green or white."

They stood there, father and son, silently looking at Ben's makeshift outfits.

"White," said his father.

Ben plucked the green shirt off his bed and hung it on his closest door, which was where he put everything he needed for the next day. He tossed the white shirt in the hamper, even though it wasn't dirty. Then the gods gave him an unexpected gift: His phone buzzed, cutting through the tension in the room.

"That's my friend Lottie," said Ben, in a tone that meant he needed some privacy.

His father took the hint and left without saying anything else.

But it wasn't a phone call. It was a notification

that Lottie had taken her Scrabble turn. She'd added MORE to Ben's NEVER.

NEVERMORE.

"Tell me about it," said Ben.

All Lined Up

Rabbit Hole: *The Rubik's Cube is three-dimensional combination puzzle invented in 1974 by Erno Rubik, a Hungarian professor of design and architecture. "If you are curious, you'll find the puzzles around you," he once said. "If you are determined, you will solve them." About 350 million Rubik's Cubes have been sold worldwide.*

Bridget's brother Gordo once went through a phase where he barked every time their dog, Sergeant, barked, which made the noise at the MacCauleys' house ten times worse, but now Gordo was nine and didn't do things like that anymore. Instead he made a pest of himself until people did what he wanted.

At the moment he was pestering Charlotte to solve his Rubik's Cube.

"Come on! Please! Please!" said Gordo, waving the Rubik's Cube in Charlotte's face while she and Bridget studied for Bridget's social studies test. They were sitting at the MacCauleys' kitchen table, learning about the Constitutional Convention. Bridget's notebook was decorated with daisies and sunflowers because she never paid attention in any of her classes except art. She preferred to daydream about her future as a famous artist in New York.

Charlotte's father once said that everyone had a "someday"—a fuzzy time in the future when life would go just as it should, every dream would come true, and things would clip along at a perfect pace. It's what got people through tough times, Mr. Lockard said. Bridget's someday had an art studio, galleries, canvases slathered in paint. Charlotte's someday was at the base of a volcano or Egyptian pyramid, where she pulled obsidian and pumice from the dirt and studied them, used tiny brushes to clean specimens, took samples to a lab, and estimated the age of cliffs and mountains.

"We're busy, *Dorko*," said Bridget. She leaned her head back and yelled, "Dad! I'm trying to learn about the Constitutional Convention, and Dorko won't leave us alone!"

The MacCauleys always yelled, even when they had no idea where anyone was in the house. Charlotte never yelled at her own house. Her mother always said, "use your inside voice," which meant speak quietly.

"Don't call your brother names!" Mac called back.

Bridget shoved Gordo away from the table, which was easy to do because he was small and wiry. He stumbled back, but rebounded right up to Charlotte again. He kept waving the Rubik's Cube. There was a thump from the next room. Donnie, probably. He was seven and always jumping off something.

"Puh-lease, Charlotte!" Gordo whined. "It only takes twenty seconds!"

Charlotte put her pen down. "Oh, all right."

"Don't!" Bridget said. "He'll never leave us alone."

"Yes, I will," Gordo said. "Just solve it one time."

Charlotte examined all sides of the Rubik's Cube while Gordo counted the seconds. The Cube was solved by the time he got to "twenty-one."

"That's one second longer than last time," he said. "You better keep practicing."

Bridget shoved him again. "You're one to talk. It'd take you twenty years to solve it!"

Gordo took the Cube and turned it around and around in his small hands. "Is your dad gonna die, Charlotte?"

Bridget gasped and gave him another hard shove. This time his butt hit the ground.

"Shut up, Gordo!" Bridget said. "God, you're such an idiot."

Gordo stood up and rubbed his behind. "I was just asking!"

"Get out of here, Dorko!"

Gordo took off down the hall, shouting to Mac

that Bridget had called him "Dorko" and "pushed him against the wall," which wasn't exactly true. But soon they could hear him playing with Donnie. They were making light-saber noises and talking about the Force.

Sergeant lumbered in and walked up to Charlotte. She scratched his ears.

"Sorry about my idiot brother," said Bridget, snapping her fingers and calling Sergeant, who walked around the table and settled at her feet.

"It's no problem," said Charlotte, even though she felt like a stone was sitting in her chest. She wanted to say: *It's not like I haven't wondered the same thing. Sometimes I think about it so much that I'm surprised there's room in my head for any other thoughts. But it's strange to hear someone say it right out loud, you know? It's like hearing your thoughts come to life when you thought they were your own. Has that ever happened to you?*

"You shouldn't give in like that," Bridget continued. "My stupid brothers need to learn that they can't always get what they want. They're spoiled enough as it is."

"I figured he would leave us alone if I just solved it real quick," Charlotte said. "It only takes a few seconds."

"Yes, we all know you're a genius and it only takes twenty seconds," Bridget mumbled.

The stone dropped from Charlotte's heart to her gut.

"Actually, twenty-one seconds," she said. She meant it to be funny, but Bridget didn't laugh. "Do you have a lot of members for the art club?" she asked, desperate to change the subject.

Bridget shrugged. "So far it's just me, Sophie, and Dee Dee." She tapped her pencil against her homework. "I asked Sophie if you could join, too, but she's the president-elect and she only wants artsy types. But you probably didn't want to join anyway."

Charlotte didn't know what to say, so she looked around the kitchen and silently made scrambles out of *Sophie Seong.*

Isophones.

Goopiness.

That's when she saw them. Near the front door, where the MacCauleys left their shoes. Charlotte's were over there, too, all lined up like a family.

Why hadn't she noticed it before?

"What's that?" she asked, pointing with her pencil.

Bridget barely turned around. "Oh. My dad got me a pair of Vans."

Charlotte curled her toes. "Seriously?"

"They're shoes," said Bridget. "Big deal."

Slow slip.

Life According to Ben

Part VIII

Sometimes the best way to start a conversation was to pretend it was already happening. Skip all the small talk. Small talk is for small people. Ben had read that somewhere. Or maybe he invented it. He couldn't remember. Nevertheless, when he called Lottie Lock that night, he said: "I have a confession."

Lottie paused. "I'm waiting."

"I wish I was taller."

A study in 2004 found that taller people were more

successful. According to *Business Insider*, a person who was six feet tall might earn $166,000 more over the course of a thirty-year career than someone who was only five feet five.

When Lottie didn't say anything, Ben said, "Your turn."

"My turn for what?"

"Confession."

Ben had on earbuds so he could play Minecraft and talk to Lottie at the same time. He was in the process of building a lake adjacent to his farmland.

His door was locked again.

"I don't have one," she said.

"Everyone has something."

"Not me."

"Okay." Ben paused. He thought about Sherry Bertrand and Purple Ribbon. "If you could change one thing about yourself, what would it be?"

"Um. Nothing."

"Nothing?"

"Nothing."

"There has to be something."

"Nah. I can't think of anything. I don't believe in that kind of stuff."

"What kind of stuff?" asked Ben. He studied his lake-in-progress from every angle.

"Changing things about yourself. You should be happy with who you are."

Ben felt warm and deeply embarrassed.

"You're right," he said, making his voice sound nonchalant as possible. "I mean, I'm tall enough anyway." Where had that come from? "I just wouldn't mind being two inches taller, like six feet." Over the course of one sentence, Ben had grown almost an entire foot. His heart beat fast, like Lottie could see him through the phone and knew he was lying.

"See?" she said. "You're good just like you are." Her voice was light, but there was something faraway about it that he didn't understand.

Girls were an endless mystery.

"How's your student-council thing going?" asked Lottie.

"Oh. It's great. Really great. I've been putting my name out there. You know. Campaigning. Making my way through the lunch crowds. I've got a whole team working for me." Now he was tall and had a campaign team?

"Wow."

"Yeah. If you wanna win, you gotta go big." He paused and let another lie roll off his tongue: "I have an insider in the attendance office. Danielle. She says I'm in the lead already. Tomorrow I'm going to fine-tune my speech."

"You have to give a speech?"

"In front of the whole school. On Friday." That part was true, at least. "I'm trying to make the most of the school experience."

There was an awkward silence that they tried to break at the same time.

"You go first," said Ben, after they stumbled over simultaneous sentences.

"I was just thinking about IQ tests."

"What about them?"

"I was thinking it would be interesting if they had tests for other things. Like, instead of an IQ test, there was a popularity test?"

"Hmm." Ben thought about all those ribbons and mall mannequins. The thumbs-up and the LSU Tigers baseball caps. "What would be on it, you think?"

"I don't know." She paused. "I guess you'd have to own the right sneakers. Something like that."

"And maybe play sports?"

"Yeah. Like soccer."

"Football."

"Chess."

They laughed.

"Hey, maybe we could start playing chess!" Images of BEN BOOT on a leaderboard danced through Ben's head, even though his chess strategy was sketchy at best. Still, if he practiced enough . . .

"Nah," said Lottie. "I'm having too much fun beating you at Scrabble."

The awkward pause returned, until Lottie said: "I thought of a confession."

"Okay. Go."

"I could eat gummy bears for the rest of my life."

"Not good for your teeth."

"I don't care," she said. "I'll get dentures."

"They should infuse gummy bears with xylitol."

"What's xylitol?"

"It's a cavity-fighting additive," said Ben. He looked at his lap and realized his hands were resting there. At some point during their brief conversation, he'd stopped working on his lake.

"X-Y-L-I-T-O-L?"

"Yep," Ben said.

"Toil, toll, till."

"Making words out of xylitol?"

"Yep."

At that moment, Ben was overwhelmed with an aching wish. He couldn't remember the last time he'd wished for something with such ferocity. It almost made him misty-eyed—almost—but he allowed himself to think it once quickly before he swallowed it away and pushed it into the corner of his mind.

I wish Lottie Lock went to my school so I'd have someone to sit with at lunch.

WEDNESDAY

hypothesis *n* : an assumption or proposed explanation made on the basis of limited evidence

Life According to Ben

Part IX

Ben was suitably dressed and full of adrenaline when he walked through the school doors the next morning, twenty minutes earlier than usual with a bag of perfectly rolled posters on his shoulder.

Mr. Higgins the security guard was sitting behind his desk at the front entrance reading a thick paperback. Ben recognized the cover, even from a distance. *Dune*.

"That's a good one," said Ben, as he walked up.

The halls were empty. His voice echoed. "What part are you on?"

"Alia's just been captured," Mr. Higgins said. He laid the book face down on the desk and raised his eyebrows. "You've read this book? It's gotta be, what, two thousand pages or so."

"The paperback is only nine hundred, if I remember correctly," Ben said. He tapped the clipboard next to the sign that said SIGN IN HERE. "I'm a student, so I'm not sure if I need to sign in or not. I came in early so I could hang up my posters." He patted his bag. "My name is Ben Boxer and I'm running for student-council treasurer. Trying to work my way up to president."

"Well, future Mr. President, be my guest," Mr. Higgins said. He waved his hand toward the empty hallway behind him.

"Thank you," said Ben.

He liked the sound of "future Mr. President," so he played it again and again in his head as he clipped through the hallways in his dress shoes. The echoes became a silent chant in his mind, like a military drill: *Future Mr. PRES-i-dent, Future Mr. PRES-i-dent.* When he reached the first blank wall in the sixth-grade hallway, he stopped, ran his hand over the cinder blocks to make sure the packing tape would stick properly, then set down his bag and pulled out a poster. Black letters. White background.

He didn't just want to be a brand. Now that he'd jumped full-force into this thing, he really wanted to implement change. He really wanted Lanester Middle School to evolve. A new mascot to replace the red-faced Indian that he found culturally offensive. Lanester Lions, maybe. More vending options. Most important: increased recycling. He wouldn't be a typical politician. He would be a consummate populist. A president for the people.

The hallway was different with no one in it. The lockers stretched on forever with their mouths closed. None of the classroom doors were open. When he yanked the first length of tape from the roll, the sound bounced off the walls. He had an urge to call out his name just so he could hear it echo, but he didn't want Mr. Higgins to come charging toward him, wondering what all the fuss was about. Plus, he didn't want to interrupt *Dune.*

Sound was a strange phenomenon. Ben thought about this as he stood on his tiptoes to hang the poster. When the hallways were full, there were too many surfaces for the sound waves to bounce from, so no echo. But now he could yell anything he wanted and hear it reverberate through the wide space around him.

Nothing makes you feel more alone than an echo.

That Minnesota Feeling

Rabbit Hole: *Many people report having feelings of dread before something terrible happens. Scientists aren't sure what causes this. Some think we receive subliminal clues without knowing it, through things like body language or peripheral vision. Others believe that our minds are constantly working through problems and solutions unconsciously, which is why we sometimes have hunches we can't explain.*

There once was this woman who lived in Minnesota. She took the same route to and from work every day. Then one August afternoon she was in her car and had a feeling something bad was going to happen, so she took an alternate route instead. Later she found out that a bridge had collapsed into the Mississippi River—the same bridge she would have taken home.

Charlotte read about her in a rabbit hole about the science of premonitions. One scientist said that some human beings had an inherent sense when something was wrong. He couldn't explain it. It was just there, like a mental beacon that stayed quiet until it suddenly perked up and sounded the alarm.

When Charlotte walked into school before the morning bell, she had one of those mental beacons. Bridget had texted her that morning to say she was running late and wouldn't be at the benches, and Charlotte's morning routine always felt weird when Bridget wasn't there. Like she was the lady who'd been cut in half at a magic show, and her head was floating around, waiting for the magician to put her back together again.

Then she saw Sophie putting stuff in her locker and decided to talk to her about the art club.

Charlotte acted like she was passing by Sophie's

locker unintentionally, even though her homeroom was in the other direction.

"Hey, Sophie," said Charlotte, smiling. She shoved her hands in her pockets, trying to look natural—or "devil-may-care," as her dad always said.

Sophie looked surprised, but smiled warmly. "Oh hey, Charlotte."

"So . . . Bridget told me about the art club."

"Oh, yeah. She comes up with the best ideas, doesn't she?"

"Yeah, she's really creative," said Charlotte. She bit her bottom lip. "I was wondering . . . I mean, I know the club's for the artsy types, but I wouldn't mind trying it. I'm not that great an artist, but it sounds fun. So maybe you'd consider letting me join, too?" She added quickly: "It could just be a trial membership."

Sophie's smile disappeared slowly. Her eyebrows furrowed in confusion.

"Oh. Um . . . ," she said. "I'm not really in charge of membership."

"I thought you were the president-elect."

"Well, kind of, I guess. We haven't officially elected officers."

"Oh."

"We're having our first meeting at lunch today," she said. She closed her locker. "I'll see what everyone thinks. You know, like if we're gonna have membership rules or something. I don't really know what the plans are."

"Sure," said Charlotte. "Thanks."

She watched Sophie walk away and immediately replayed the conversation in her head, like a premonition.

She comes up with the best ideas, doesn't she?

But Bridget had said the art club was Sophie's idea.

Anyway, premonitions were for things that hadn't happened yet, not stuff from yesterday.

It didn't mean anything.

Who cares whose idea it was?

You're thinking too much, Charlotte told herself. *That's all.*

Life According to Ben

Part X

Middle school was overrun with plastic water bottles, but Ben couldn't bring himself to drink from disposable materials. Not when every square mile of the ocean contained more than forty-six thousand pieces of plastic. So he brought a reusable bottle from home and filled it with water from the school fountain, which tasted like he'd shoved a handful of pennies in his mouth, but he needed to stay well hydrated for the big speech on Friday.

He had just closed his locker and taken a big swig of coppery water when Theo and a group of like-minded boys (including Derrick Whatshisname) sauntered up to him. Theo's expression reminded Ben of something from *The Chamber of Secrets*: Severus Snape standing in black robes, smiling in a way that told Harry he and Ron were in very deep trouble.

Theo wasn't wearing a black robe, but still.

"Hey, Benny," said Theo, standing right across from him. Ben wondered if he would be shoved into his locker. Isn't that the kind of stuff that happened in moments like this? "Nice tie."

Yes, it was. His mother had bought it for a mathlete competition the previous year. Both of his parents had watched Ben take first place that day. Afterward they ate at the Olive Garden. They told Ben he could order whatever he wanted, so he got lobster ravioli. He remembered the ravioli, but he couldn't remember what they talked about over dinner.

He should have been paying more attention.

"I hear they're serving *shrimp* for lunch today," Theo said.

The boys laughed. But the joke was on them. They would never serve shellfish in the cafeteria, not with the potential for food poisoning. Millions of Americans had food allergies and shellfish was the most common. Not to mention the cost.

Only.

"Do you play any sports?" asked Theo.

Ben thought of his conversation with Lottie the night before. Soccer. Football. Chess. He knew better than to say "chess," but he didn't know enough to say something else. So he stood there.

"Do you know how to play basketball?" asked Theo.

"Uh," said Ben.

Theo stretched his neck and said, "Let me teach you how to dribble."

And suddenly Ben felt Theo's hand on his forehead. It was a strange feeling, like having a cockroach crawl across your toes or feeling the pinch of a hermit crab on the soft part of your foot. Only this didn't feel like a crawl or a pinch. Theo's hand was clammy and it was only there for a moment, enough to push Ben's head back until it slammed into the locker. Then it was gone.

"That's how you dribble," Theo said.

Ben's ears rang from the impact. A sudden headache shot from the back of his head to his eyes as Theo and his friends disappeared into the crowded hallway. Ben thought the sound of his head hitting the locker was the loudest crash on earth. It buzzed through every part of his body. But no one else seemed fazed. Middle-school hallways were full of so much activity. Who would notice such a small little thing?

Not Proud

Rabbit Hole: *Henry VIII, the last Tudor king, had figures of himself carved into the eaves of the Great Hall at Hampton Court. The early sixteenth century was a time of great turmoil and unrest for the paranoid king. The "eavesdroppers" were meant to discourage gossip.*

Charlotte had never been so ashamed to stand in the nonfiction section in her life.

Nonfiction was directly behind the collection of tables in the school library where Charlotte knew Bridget and the art club would meet. Bridget, like most humans, was a creature of habit. Charlotte knew she would sit at the four-top near the books about the Civil War. Charlotte had been to the library with Bridget dozens of times and she always chose the same table. So here Charlotte was, pretending to be completely enthralled by American history, waiting for the club to show up.

Charlotte was in disguise. Well, sort of. She had one earbud in—muted—and she slouched her shoulders in a general pretense of nonchalance. In other words: She was acting casual. If she were discovered, she would pretend to be totally surprised. *What a coincidence,* she would say.

She wasn't proud of herself.

In fact, she felt pathetic.

Charlotte couldn't see the library doors from where she was standing, but they were heavy and had a push bar so she could hear when they opened. If the art club sat at the tables nearest the windows, they would be too far away, but if she knew Bridget, she would sit right within earshot. Charlotte peered through the books—casual, casual—and hoped no one snagged the spot.

Sure enough, Bridget walked in and sat at her table. Charlotte saw the back of her head. Sophie and Dee Dee sat directly across from her.

Charlotte pulled a book from the shelf and opened it like she was reading. A grainy black-and-white picture of a man with a bushy mustache stared back at her. According to the caption his name was LaFayette C. Baker.

I know what you're doing, weirdo, his eyes said.

Charlotte made word scrambles out of *LaFayette* while Bridget called the meeting to order.

Featly.

Fettle.

Latte.

"I talked to Charlotte this morning," Sophie said. Her voice sounded apologetic. Maybe she regretted making the club so exclusive. "She asked if she could join."

Blood rushed in Charlotte's ears.

"What did you say?" asked Bridget.

Sophie didn't answer. At least, not that Charlotte could hear.

"I can't believe she talked to you," Bridget said.

She's right. I should've made my case directly to Bridget, Charlotte thought. *She's my best friend, after all. Even if she's going to Red's and wearing Vans.*

Then again, so was Charlotte. She'd convinced her mother to buy her a pair. The sneakers had been rubbing blisters into both heels for the past hour.

"Why don't we just let her join?" said Dee Dee. "It might be good to have one of the TAG kids in the group. She could . . . I don't know, come up with smart stuff for the club."

"It's no big deal to me, either," Sophie said.

They were both looking at Bridget.

Charlotte got a sinking feeling in her gut.

"Ugh," Bridget groaned. "Why does she have to make things so awkward?"

Charlotte looked at the guy with the mustache. She suddenly felt very stupid, naive, and clueless. She also felt pathetic. Stupid, naive, clueless, and pathetic.

She felt exposed, too, even though she knew they couldn't see her.

"She's like a parasite, I swear," said Bridget. "I feel bad saying it, but it's true."

Charlotte had heard Bridget say those same words about other kids so many times. *Dee Dee is such a terrible gossip. I feel bad saying it, but it's true. Sophie wears too much makeup sometimes and it makes her look trashy. I feel bad saying it, but it's true.*

Dee Dee yawned. "She doesn't seem that bad to me."

"Don't you think it's kind of desperate how she waited until you were alone to talk to you?" Bridget said to Sophie. "It's like she went behind my back or something."

Sophie shrugged. "I guess."

"I know I'm being a terrible friend saying this,

especially since her dad is in the hospital, but lately I've felt like a babysitter," said Bridget. "It's like . . . I don't know. We don't have anything in common anymore."

"You're not a terrible friend," said Sophie. "You're just being honest."

"I didn't know her dad was in the hospital," said Dee Dee.

"Yeah. He had a heart attack. Her parents are ancient, so it was bound to happen sometime. He was driving when it happened." She paused. "He crashed into Old Navy and almost killed like three people in the process."

That last part wasn't true.

Charlotte's body was on fire. The heat came in an instant, like she'd stepped into an oven. She didn't want to listen anymore, but she couldn't stop.

Dee Dee gasped. Charlotte could hear the news traveling through the school hallways now, growing as it went. *Did you know Charlotte's dad had a massive heart attack while he was driving, and he flew off the overpass and landed on top of a tractor-trailer and killed seventy-five people?*

All those times Charlotte had confided in Bridget about her dad's heart, and his pills, and how she worried because her parents were older than everyone else's, and Bridget had said over and over that it didn't matter, everything would be okay. "Sure, your parents will be around when you graduate from high school and college," Bridget had said. "They'll be there when you get married. Sure."

"I know I sound harsh, but I can't take it anymore," said Bridget. "How do you break up with friends, anyway? Is it the same as breaking up with boyfriends?"

As if Bridget would know. She'd never had a boyfriend. Over the summer she'd said she didn't want to graduate from middle school as the only girl who'd never been kissed. Charlotte had said, "I won't kiss anyone either, then. You won't be alone." And Bridget had just rolled her eyes and said, "Of course you won't. That's not what I'm talking about." At the time Charlotte had wondered: *What are you talking about, then?* Middle school seemed like an endless aching game where everyone knew the rules but her.

"It doesn't matter," Sophie said. "You can't break up with a friend when they're going through a hard time like that. It wouldn't be right. Wait until her dad feels better, and then you can just kinda . . . drift apart."

"Yeah, but where is she gonna drift?" Bridget said. "She doesn't have any other friends." She paused. "I mean, she has a rock collection. She even has a rock that she uses as a lucky charm. It's just so . . . immature. You know?"

Charlotte wondered how many atoms existed in the library, because it felt like each one of them carried Bridget's voice with it. *She even has a rock that she uses as a lucky charm.* Every corner, every book, every molecule of air absorbed *immature* and *parasite* and *bound to happen.*

She thought of Sphinx sitting dutifully in its place and all the times it'd been clutched inside Bridget's palm.

"Wait. She has a pet rock?" asked Dee Dee.

"Well . . ." Bridget considered this then giggled. "Kinda."

Her best friend was laughing. At her.

And the other girls laughed, too.

Charlotte wanted to sweep all the stupid nonfiction books off the shelf and scream. She wanted to tell the so-called art club that *Bridget* was the one who had named Sphinx. That *Bridget* had wished on that rock dozens—maybe hundreds—of times. She wanted them to know that her rock collection was anything but immature. Did *they* know what a turquenite was? Could *they* pick an aventurine out of a lineup? Could *they* define igneous differentiation and fractional crystallization?

The conversation at the table shifted to more interesting gossip. Hannah Miller and Milo Adiga had broken up, and "no one could believe it," according to Dee Dee.

Charlotte only had a faint idea who Hannah and Milo were. Bridget knew, though. She was one of the people who couldn't believe it. And then she talked about how cute Milo Adiga was, and the so-called art club launched into a series of plans and strategies for them to meet.

When had Bridget met all these people?

When did she decide Milo was cute?

Charlotte tried to imagine herself sitting there, talking about Hannah and Milo, and which boys at West were the cutest. Charlotte thought the boys at West smelled like sweat. They were loud. They made stupid jokes. They weren't like Mateo. They weren't even like Ben Boot, that much she knew.

Charlotte sitting at the art club table?

Did not compute.

Life According to Ben

Part XI

Millions of tons of debris were floating around in the earth's seas, threatening and killing marine life. Ben had nightmares about this sometimes. Manatees smothered by grocery bags. Dolphins muzzled by plastic six-pack rings. Whales swallowing take-out containers.

Ben had planned to spend his lunch period working on his speech, but he'd become too distracted by items going in the wrong bins and it occurred to him that he could do something about it and meet people at the same time. So he decided to stand between the trash and recyclable receptacles wearing his friendliest smile.

It bewildered Ben that no one at Lanester seemed remotely interested in the "ocean of garbage," as he liked to call it, but he figured it was because they weren't fully educated on the issues. He was going to take care of that and woo potential voters at the same time. Multitasking. He refused to let Theo, Sherry, Derrick Whatshisname, or anyone else deter him. Adversity built character. It was all part of politics.

"Focus on the greater good," he whispered, under his breath.

As far as Ben could tell, the biggest problem with the cafeteria bins was that the students threw their plastics into the bin for trash, rather than the other way around.

"This one is for recyclables," said Ben to the first person who walked up—a girl with a T-shirt that said

FUTURE DIVA, who was about to drop an empty Coke can into the trash.

She gave him a quizzical look, but beelined to the right bin.

"Thank you," said Ben. "My name is Ben Boxer and I'm running for student council."

He continued this routine as more students walked up, but added statistics for good measure.

"Excuse me," he said. "I'm Ben Boxer and I'm running for student council. Did you know that millions of milk jugs are introduced into our oceans each year?"

He varied the stats as more students streamed through.

"Twenty billion plastic bottles are tossed into the trash annually."

"At least one hundred thousand marine creatures died from plastic entanglement last year."

For the most part he got bewildered looks and some laughter, but he felt a sense of accomplishment anyway because so far his strategy was working—sixth graders watched him curiously as he gestured frantically toward the appropriate bin, but they would realize their error and discard properly.

There were so many people he didn't know. Like there were two schools: one with Ben and another with every else.

Which universe? Pluto?

When Theo and his friends walked up, Ben absently touched the back of his head and watched them throw all their paper and plastic into the trash. He clamped his mouth shut and made no eye contact, but no matter.

"How's it going, *prawn*?" said Theo. The other boys snickered. "Do you know what a *prawn* is?"

Ben shifted his eyes toward Mrs. Fausto, the English teacher, who was on lunch duty. She stood near the windows and glanced around the room like an attentive cat, ready to pounce. But she wasn't watching Ben. Not at that moment, anyway.

"A prawn is a shrimp," said Theo. Pause. "Hey, you have something on your shirt."

Ben fought the urge to check.

"It's right there," Theo continued. "You see it?" He pressed a finger against Ben's chest, hard enough to make him stumble back. And he was right: Ben *did* have something on his shirt. Now. Theo's finger had been slathered in ketchup.

"You oughta do something about that," Theo said.

He turned and walked off with the other boys trailing behind him.

Ben stared at the smear in bewilderment then abandoned his post to approach Mrs. Fausto, whose attention was focused on a nearby table.

"Excuse me," he said. "I seem to have ketchup on my shirt."

Mrs. Fausto turned toward him and frowned at the smear.

"Certainly appears that way," she said.

"Do you have any club soda?" Ben asked.

"Sorry, no club soda. But you could try soaking it in warm water. Stop by the attendance office. They have spirit shirts you can wear."

"What's a spirit shirt?"

"You'll see."

Ben thought of the last time he'd been in the attendance office. Danielle Carlile had said he'd make a good representative. He hoped she wouldn't remember him, but she did.

"Ben Boxer, as I live and breathe," she said. She was sitting at her desk. There was a boy in the office, too, standing behind the sign-in/sign-out sheet.

"May I help you?" he asked, with forced enthusiasm.

"I'm inquiring about spirit shirts," said Ben.

"What about them?" said the boy.

"Do you have any?" Ben stepped back and indicated the ketchup. "I accidentally dropped ketchup on my shirt."

The boy leaned forward and narrowed his tired eyes. "Looks like a bolt of lightning."

"Yes!" Ben's face lit up. "That's what I thought! Well, to be more specific, I thought it looked like Harry Potter's scar."

"Same thing."

"Agreed." Ben drummed his fingers on the counter. "Now about those spirit shirts?"

"Oh, yeah. Hang on." The boy disappeared into a back closet. The sound of Mrs. Carlile clicking the mouse filled the room.

"You should get some music in here," Ben suggested.

"That would be way too exciting," Mrs. Carlile said.

The boy came back with shirts draped over each arm.

"What's your size?" he asked.

Ben held out his arms like he was being measured by an invisible tailor. "Medium."

The boy tossed a shirt to Ben, who failed to catch it. He bent over and picked it up. That's when he realized what a "spirit shirt" was. It was bright red. Across the front it said: GO LANESTER!! in fat, white letters. Ben didn't think the additional exclamation mark was necessary. There was a rather large and colorful drawing of the mascot on the front. It said WE'RE NO 1!! on the back.

Ben groaned. "This is monstrous." He held it up. "And it says we're no one."

"I think it's 'we're number one.'"

"There should be a period after *N-O*, then. Otherwise it says we're no one."

"They should've gone with the number sign," Mrs. Carlile said. "And no mascot. Blame the spirit committee."

Ben scrunched his nose. "Beggars can't be choosers, I guess."

"I guess," said the boy, still holding the other shirts. He looked like a coatrack.

Ben smiled wide. "Thank you, Mr.—?"

"My name is Wyatt," said the boy.

"Thank you, Wyatt," said Ben.

Wyatt shrugged.

Ben leaned forward and motioned for Wyatt to come closer.

"How'd you get this gig?" Ben asked.

"Gig?"

"This job, in the office."

"Oh," said Wyatt. "My mom doesn't want me anywhere near the cafeteria, so I come here during lunch. I eat my sandwich and assist Mrs. Carlile with stuff. Mostly I just stand here and say 'May I help you?'"

"Why doesn't your mom want you anywhere near the cafeteria? I know the food's bad, but it's not toxic or anything." Ben usually had a small salad from the salad bar. There was never a line at the salad bar, so he could get his food and keep moving.

"It's toxic for me," said Wyatt. "I'm allergic."

"To the cafeteria?"

"Not specifically. More like the stuff in the cafeteria. Peanuts—well, any kind of nuts, actually—milk, soy.

If a peanut comes anywhere near me, my throat starts swelling up."

Ben's eyes widened. "Anaphylactic shock."

Wyatt snapped his fingers. "Bingo."

"Your inflammatory mediators and cytokines react inappropriately to what they perceive as dangerous pathogens."

"Basically."

"Interesting," said Ben.

Wyatt shrugged. "I guess."

Ben straightened up and half waved. "Well. See you around."

"Yeah," said Wyatt. "See you around."

Ben carried his shirt to the boys' bathroom knowing the medium would be too big. But it's not often that you're given a choice of what you want to be, and Ben decided he didn't want to be small.

Pick Something Real

Rabbit Hole: *Some human tears contain natural painkillers. That's why people often feel better after a good cry. One international study found that the most popular place and time to cry is at home, between seven and ten p.m. Thirty-five percent of people reported that they cried alone.*

When they were in fourth grade, Bridget and Charlotte liked to sit facing each other on the floor of Charlotte's bedroom with their feet pressed together and legs outstretched. They would sit like that for hours, asking each other questions. There were only two rules: You had to tell the truth and everything was secret. It was like an endless game of Truth or Dare, except there were no dares.

"What was your most embarrassing moment?" That was one of the questions. Bridget said that hers was when she'd tripped over a display case in science class and fallen flat on her face in front of everyone.

"Mine was when I misspelled *aerial* at the school spelling bee," Charlotte had said. "I choked and forgot the *e*." She had watched her mother cringe when they rang the bell. "Then Tori Baraldi won."

Bridget shook her head. "That's not even embarrassing. Pick something real."

But it *had* been real to Charlotte.

If they were to sit on the floor of her bedroom now and put their feet together, Charlotte knew what she'd say.

The time you called me a parasite and I ran to the bathroom after the bell to cry in a stall alone. I had to call my mom and pretend I was sick so she could pick me up from school.

Charlotte was home now, in bed, clutching Sphinx. Her head ached. Her eyes burned.

Her mom knocked on the door.

"Are you okay?" she asked. "Do you need anything?"

"I'm fine, Mom," Charlotte said. Her voice sounded stuffy and hoarse, like it came from someone else.

"I'm going to the hospital soon. Do you want to come with me?"

What about it, Charlotte? What kind of daughter are you, anyway? Your father is in ICU and you haven't even gone to see him. You keep thinking about starfish and scalpels and Scrabble collecting dust in the closet. But you still haven't walked into the room. You haven't gone over the threshold. Why?

Charlotte squeezed her eyes as tightly shut as she could.

"I better not," she said. She coughed. "Since I'm sick and everything."

Her mother paused. Charlotte felt her presence on the other side of the door.

There was a part of Charlotte that wanted to say more. *Remember when Bridget would spend the night, and Dad would let us watch scary movies even though you said it wasn't okay, and then you'd tell us funny jokes before bed so we wouldn't have nightmares? And remember that time the four of us played Scrabble and you told Bridget that her play was "very clever," and I got jealous but I smiled anyway because Bridget looked so proud? And remember when you made us those hippie costumes for Halloween and told us stories about the seventies and played some of your old songs on the record player, and me and Bridget danced and danced and laughed and laughed?*

Well, things have changed.

Dad isn't home and you don't know Bridget anymore.

"Okay," her mother said. "I'll be back soon. Text if you need anything."

Her mom didn't need to hear her problems, and Charlotte wouldn't know where to start anyway.

There were slow slips everywhere.

Charlotte didn't open her eyes until her phone buzzed.

Ben had played MASCOT.

At least there was something she could still count on.

Life According to Ben

Part XII

Ben tapped his finger against his reusable water bottle and listened to the *plink, plink, plink* as his eyes ran over the laptop screen. No Minecraft tonight. It was time to write the best speech since Gettysburg. Theo, Sherry, Derrick, and all their minions would regret the day they had underestimated his powers of persuasion. If he didn't win the election, he would at least give a resounding speech that would shake Lanester Middle School to its core. The stage would be his spotlight. His moment in the sun. The apex of his evolution. He would be a finch flying out of the darkness.

But first he needed words.

So far all he had were jokes. According to the internet, it was smart to open a speech with laughter. It relaxed the audience and the speaker. And he had three jokes to choose from, all of which were school related.

1. If sleep is good for the brain, how come they don't let us sleep in school? (Ben thought this could have mass appeal, even though he couldn't imagine falling asleep in class.)

2. Question: What's a teacher's favorite nation? Answer: Expla-nation. (Ben thought this was pretty funny, but he worried about offending the teachers. He wasn't sure if it was offensive or not. He didn't think so.)

3. Question: What did one math book say to the other? Answer: Don't bother me, I've got my own problems! (Ben considered this the winner thus far. It was funnier than the first and didn't poke fun at anyone.)

After the laughter died down, he would introduce himself and give a rundown of his qualifications. He only had four minutes, so the introduction would be brief. One minute, tops. The most important part of the campaign isn't the candidate, but what that candidate plans to do. He didn't want to be a politician who ran on charisma alone. All sizzle, no steak. He would be the sizzle *and* the steak. The bulk of his talk would revolve around his vision for Lanester Middle School. Ways to help the students, teachers, and administration make it the best it could be. He knew that some of his ideas were a long shot—replacing all individual desks with collaborative tables, for example—but he would offer them nonetheless.

Sometimes you have to think big and take small steps. No one got anywhere by thinking small.

He numbered his platform proposals one through eleven and wrote them out in detail. Each time he finished a sentence, he heard Theo's voice (*What environment? Pluto?*) and saw Sherry Bertrand's face (*Be my guest*). But he would not be defeated. He would not relinquish control over his own emotional well-being. He only had himself now—no more reliable parental units to have his back.

"You are a finch," he said, without looking away from his laptop. "You are a finch."

He tried to find solace in the fact that Theo Barrett was his tormentor instead of, say, Albert Einstein or Stephen Hawking. Theo Barrett was clearly no Einstein. And Sherry? Well, clearly Sherry had nursed a long-held grudge against him. But she had been wrong, hadn't she? You weren't supposed to cheat—right? Maybe Ben could have handled it better, but he knew how hard Kyle had studied for that test, and it didn't seem right for her to just take his answers. It didn't seem like justice. He had done the right thing—hadn't he?

"You are a finch," he repeated. *"You are a finch."*

What environment? Pluto?

Ben touched the back of his head, expecting to feel a knot. He didn't.

He picked up his phone.

"I have news," he said, when Lottie answered. He didn't know what news he was going to tell her. His parents' divorce? His theories of personal evolution? The situation with Sherry, Theo, and the rest?

He only knew that he wanted to say something to someone about something.

"Have you conquered the school already?" she said. "Because it's your turn and you haven't gone yet."

She sounded stuffy. Sick, maybe.

"I've been busy preparing my speech," Ben said. "Are you sick? You sound sick."

"Yeah. I had to leave school today. Fever and stuff."

He thought about the sign-in/sign-out sheet and wondered if Lottie's school had a kid like Wyatt manning it.

"You know," said Ben. "Chicken soup isn't just an old wives' tale. Science shows that it actually helps reduce upper respiratory cold symptoms."

"I'll keep that in mind." She sniffled. "Actually, I think I have news, too."

Ben leaned back in his chair. "You go first."

"Well . . . ," said Lottie. "I don't know. Never mind. It's stupid."

"No it's not."

"How do you know? I haven't even told you yet."

"If it's news to you, then it isn't stupid."

"It's not really news, I guess. More like a problem."

"Excellent. I love problems."

She took a deep breath. "The thing is . . . I don't want to be friends with my best friend anymore and I don't know how to tell her."

Uh-oh. This was a problem of the social variety.

He wasn't so good at solving those.

"What happened?" he asked. "Did you get in a fight?"

Lottie paused. "Sort of. It's just . . . she can be irritating sometimes, you know? Always hanging around me. Stuff like that. She doesn't have many other friends. I'm kinda the only one. And it gets to be too much. There are other people I want to hang out with."

"Why don't you just all hang out together?" asked Ben.

"I don't know if she'd mix well with my other friends."

"You should let them decide. Maybe she'll find friends in the group, too."

"Yeah," said Lottie. "Maybe."

Then again, I may not know what I'm talking about, Ben thought. *It's not like I'm drowning in friends over here.*

Lottie was quiet for a long time. So long, in fact, that Ben wondered if she was still there.

When she finally spoke, her voice was tight and heavy.

"What was your news?" she asked.

Ben picked up his pencil and tapped the water bottle again. *Plink, plink, plink.*

"I might be moving to Ann Arbor," said Ben. "It's in Michigan."

"Cool. I've never been to Michigan, but it scrambles to *chiming*. Like bells. So maybe that's a good sign." She sniffled again.

"Maybe," said Ben.

They were both quiet.

"Well," he said. "Good luck with your friend."

"Good luck with your Michigan," she replied.

THURSDAY

rhetorical *adj* : **1** : asked in order to produce an effect or make a statement
2 : a question without a real answer

River

Rabbit Hole: *A group of tortoises is called a creep. A group of camels is called a caravan. A group of wolves is called a pack. Although wolves tend to travel together, one member is occasionally ostracized and becomes a "lone wolf." Life is difficult for lone wolves, but their self-reliance often makes them stronger than average.*

"Your father is doing really well," said Charlotte's mother.

Normally Charlotte walked to school, but it was raining. Sheets and sheets that backed up traffic and turned Hampshire into a river. Her mother drove slowly even in nice weather; in the rain, she moved like a tortoise. Most of the time it made Charlotte crazy and she had to resist the urge to lean over and step on the gas herself, even though she'd never driven a car before. But she was thankful for it today. She didn't want to get to school early. She didn't want to face the benches.

She'd cried so much the night before that she soaked her pillow. When she woke up, her cheek was damp and itched. She was pretty sure she'd been crying about Bridget, but as the night went on she had thought about her father and even her mother—how her mother hadn't hassled her about going to see her dad and had been unusually patient—and then a million of other things crept into her mind. Scalpels and YouTube videos of open-heart surgeries. Starfish dissections. And things that didn't make any sense. Her parents looking at the ballroom ceiling. Her hidden dolls. Scrabble on the dining room table. Staring at Gauguin and wondering when she could leave. Ben

Boot, too, and the things he said on the phone—*Why don't you just all hang out together?*—and after a while she wasn't sure what she was crying about.

Were there other people out there who had so many things to cry about that they didn't know which one to choose?

"They'll move him to a regular room soon. Maybe tomorrow," continued her mother. "He'll look more like himself then."

Charlotte wanted to ask if he'd asked where she was. If so, what did her mother tell him? But she was afraid to open her mouth, afraid that she'd only start crying again. She wondered what Ann Arbor looked like. She wished she was going somewhere, too. She wished she had good news like Ben.

Life According to Ben

Part XIII

". . . and that is why I'd love to have your vote for student council."

Ben bowed without taking his eyes off his mother, who was sitting at full attention on the couch. Ben had once read that up to 93 percent of communication is nonverbal, so he wanted to make sure he caught every nuance of her response. She'd been difficult to read—ever since the devolution, she'd developed a new set of facial expressions—but after his bow she set her morning coffee on the side table and clapped like he'd just performed at Carnegie Hall.

"That was perfect," she said.

Ben took this with a grain of salt. She often said everything he did was "perfect," which he knew couldn't be true, even if he wished it were. He wondered what she would think if she knew her perfect son was getting his head slammed into lockers. What would she say about him having condiments slathered on his shirt? The warm water hadn't even fixed it. The shirt was now buried at the bottom of his wastebasket, under crumpled speech notes.

He was, as Sherry Bertrand put it, the "biggest dork in school," so maybe he was good at something, after all. *I'm so proud of my perfect Ben. The other children think he's the biggest dork in school. Isn't that marvelous?*

"It can't be perfect," he said, flatly. "Nothing's perfect."

"Except my perfect pineapple," she said.

This was an old pet name. Something she used to

call him years ago, when everything was different. A feeling tugged inside him. He couldn't tell what it was, exactly. Some of it was anger. If his parents were going to devolve the family, they shouldn't be able to pretend things were the same when everything had changed. His father left early in the morning and came home late at night. There were boxes covertly tucked in corners with some of his things inside. His mother watched *Make Me Famous* alone. And Ben locked his bedroom door.

"I'm serious," said Ben. "It's not like FDR's mother called him 'perfect pineapple' when he ran against Hoover."

"We don't know that."

Ben tightened his lips into a line and glared at her.

"Okay," Mrs. Boxer said. "Try not to be quite so robotic when you move your arms. It looks rehearsed."

"I look robotic?"

She picked up her coffee. "Slightly robotic."

"I'll have to work on my hand gestures. Make them

more fluid." He tried moving his arms as naturally as possible. "Good feedback."

"Make sure you drink plenty of water to stay hydrated. You don't want your mouth to go dry."

"I always drink the recommended daily amount."

"And don't eat a big breakfast or you'll get an upset stomach."

"I'll have toast."

"And take deep breaths just before."

"I know, Mom." Ben stopped practicing his hand gestures. He smoothed down his khakis and straightened his tie. He stood as tall as possible. "How do I look? This is my last day before the speech to make a good impression."

He knew what she was going to say before she said it.

"Perfect," she said.

Nows

Rabbit Hole: *Murphy's Law was named after Edward Murphy, an aerospace engineer. He claimed that the best way to prepare for something was to understand all the worst-case scenarios. It's also a good idea to be alert to the best-case scenarios, too.*

Here was how you avoid your best friend in the morning: You don't make it to the morning bench. You take your time putting your books away so you don't cross paths in the hallway. If she texts to ask where you are, you don't answer—but in this case it doesn't matter, because she doesn't.

But now there was lunch.

The tree was there, of course. Tall and looming. Had it always been so big? Why hadn't she noticed? The branches stretched like arms, hovering over the patch of grass where she and Bridget always sat. The leaves created a natural umbrella of shade.

Charlotte wasn't sure what she was going to do, so she went through the motions on autopilot. She got her chips and soda and made her way to the usual spot.

Tori and her friends were standing off to the side, chatting in their own spot—near the soccer goal—and as soon as they saw her approach, they turned toward her like a multiheaded beast. That's when the laces of her new Vans—laces that were stupidly long, but supposedly fashionable at West Middle School, at least for the moment—tangled themselves under her feet. She fell hard. Her chips flew out of her hand and landed about ten feet away. Her soda, too. The wind was knocked out of her lungs. Her knee hit a pebble and a pinch went up her leg. She reached for a hand-up then realized no one was offering, so she stood on her own. Her knee burned against her jeans and she knew she had a cut.

"Well done, Lock-nerd!" Tori called, laughing. She clapped.

The clapping spread to Milo Adiga—Charlotte thought it was Milo Adiga, anyway—who watched Charlotte struggle to stand up. A group of boys were with him, but none of them made a move.

Charlotte made a promise to herself then and there: *If I ever see someone fall, I'll ask if they're okay.*

"Such a loser," said Tori to Isabelle Meade.

Charlotte knew Isabelle. She used to, at least. Charlotte had gone to her birthday party in third grade. Isabelle had come to Charlotte's party, too. Her dad kept saying, "What's the biz, Izz?" and they all giggled like it was the funniest thing they'd ever heard.

"No wonder no one likes her," Isabelle said.

Charlotte's jeans were scuffed and muddy. Tiny scrapes lined the heels of her hands. The sun shone directly overhead. *Look over here, everyone! Look at this clumsy idiot! She has no friends and she can't even walk straight! No wonder no one likes her.*

Charlotte had the sudden urge to cry. It was stronger than any force she'd ever felt before, and it seemed inevitable that she would succumb in front of everyone. But she managed to hold herself together. Just.

She left her chips and soda behind when she limped away.

And she's a litterbug!

She didn't know where she was going until she got there.

The ladder next to the Dumpster.

She and Bridget had discovered the ladder on the first day of sixth grade. They had spent two whole days daring each other to climb it.

"Let's climb it," Bridget had said. She turned her head this way and that to see if anyone was coming. "Maybe we'll be able to look through vents and see everything in school. Maybe we'll be able to see into the boys' locker room."

Bridget giggled. Charlotte scrunched her nose.

The ladder was out of sight, in a corner by the gym, half-hidden by the Dumpster. Charlotte couldn't remember now what had brought them there.

"Come on," Bridget had urged. "You go first."

But Charlotte hadn't climbed it then. She didn't want to get caught. Her mother had given her a big speech about the struggles of middle school and she didn't want to end her first day in the principal's office.

"You're such a prude sometimes," Bridget had said.

But she didn't climb up, either.

Charlotte hadn't thought of the ladder since, but that's where her feet went now. She climbed it without thinking. Her hands hurt. Her knees, too. But she didn't stop until she was on the roof.

She'd never been on a roof before. She wasn't

exactly a roof-climbing type of person. But here she was.

Everything was different from this vantage point. Not in a good way or a bad way.

Just different.

She sat cross-legged and watched the seventh graders putter around like ants. There were Milo and his friends, standing in a wide circle. Milo snuck up behind one of the other boys and kneed him in the back of the leg, trying to get him to fall, but it didn't work. The other boy—maybe his name was Ian—turned around and punched Milo in the arm.

Charlotte didn't understand why any girl, much less Bridget, would think these boys were cute.

The treetops were incredible from up here—yellows, reds, oranges, and greens. She knew there were houses and neighborhoods to her left, but all she could see were trees in that direction. If not for the noise of the kids outside, she could pretend there were no people there at all.

Someday, I'll be digging for specimens in Egyptian pyramids and none of this will matter.

But for now, it did.

She looked for her chips and soda in the grass, but couldn't find them.

No wonder no one likes her.

The heat materialized quickly so she moved to the long rectangle of shade cast by the air conditioner and stretched out on the roof. It was dirty and sprinkled with dried leaves, but so what? She stared up, up at the sky and squinted. She saw three white clouds. One of them looked like a rabbit wearing a cape. The sky was a perfect shade of blue.

A symphony of blue and yellow.

After staring at the sky for too long, Charlotte's eyes started to play tricks on her, like she was going blind, but only for a moment. She squeezed them shut and sat up. She was dizzy. She opened her eyes slowly and blinked, blinked, blinked. When she focused again, she was staring at the AC unit.

Someone had written on it in permanent marker.

IN THREE WORDS I CAN SUM UP EVERYTHING I KNOW ABOUT LIFE:

____________ ____________ ____________

Charlotte looked around, as if a person was still there with a marker, even though she could tell it had been written a long time ago.

What were the three words?

"Hey."

Charlotte jumped, startled. She turned and saw a hazy silhouette. She recognized the uneven socks.

"Hey," said Charlotte. "What are you doing up here?"

Magda sat down in the shade next to her. A sheen of sweat covered her face. She had a lunchbox—the same one she'd had in fifth grade—plain yellow—and set it next to her.

"I could ask you the same thing," she said. She

nodded toward her lunchbox. "This is where I eat lunch."

Charlotte almost asked why, but then realized she knew the answer.

"I like it up here," said Magda. "When I grow up, I'm going to live in a penthouse. Like, the topmost apartment somewhere. Just so I can look out the window and see everything from a hundred stories up. I won't even need furniture."

Charlotte tried to picture Magda in a fancy apartment. She couldn't.

She cleared her throat.

"My dad says everyone has a big someday. A dream, I guess. Of what they want their life to be," said Charlotte. "I guess that's yours."

They stared out at the other kids, bustling around like ants.

"Emily Dickinson once said 'forever is composed of Nows,'" said Magda.

"You know a lot about poetry," Charlotte said. She

turned to the treetops. "I like it up here, too. It makes things look different."

"If you don't see anything beautiful, change your viewpoint," said Magda.

"Which poet said that?"

"Magda Rivera." Magda leaned forward, picked up a wayward leaf, and held it up to her phone to take a picture. After a few seconds the app gave her an answer, and she said, "Dogwood."

"I should tell my dad about that app," Charlotte said. "He'd probably like it."

Magda put her phone in her back pocket. "He already has it. He's the one who told me about it."

"Really?" Charlotte didn't know her dad downloaded apps.

"Yeah. I was outside one day, making a leaf rubbing—have you ever done that? Where you put a piece of paper over a leaf and color a pencil over it? Anyway, I was doing one of those and he came over to say hi then he told me all about the trees in our yard. It was cool. And he showed me the app."

Charlotte pictured it. *Here is the pear tree, Magda. And this is a pine and a cherry blossom. See?*

He'd never talked about trees to Charlotte.

Then again, she hadn't paid much attention lately.

A knot formed in her throat.

She swallowed it away.

Life According to Ben

Part XIV

"Ben Boxer, as I live and—ohmygod!"

Mrs. Carlile stood up at her desk.

Wyatt leaned forward and squinted. "Dude," he said. "What happened?

"I took a tumble on the way to the cafeteria," said Ben. He forced a shrug. He knew he was bleeding, but hadn't looked in a mirror. "Clumsy me."

This was a lie, of course. Well, not totally. He *did* take a tumble. It just happened to be over Theo Barrett's sneaker. Ben had never realized how easy it was to trip someone without anyone else noticing. You just stick your foot in the right place and watch the person fall. It doesn't take much. And if it's done with exceptional skill, your witnesses are few. In this case, Derrick and Sherry. And they weren't the most sympathetic people on the planet. When Ben fell—books flying, chin hitting the pavement—they laughed. It was such a cliché getting tripped by a bully. That's what popped into Ben's head as he fell.

No one stopped to offer Ben a hand. Everyone walked around him on their way to lunch or wherever. Ben collected his books, hid his chin behind *Advanced Concepts in Math*, and went straight for the attendance office. If they had spirit shirts, maybe they had Band-Aids—right?

Mrs. Carlile waved toward Wyatt. "Get the first-aid kit from the closet. We'll get it cleaned up." She motioned for Ben to come to her desk.

Standing on the opposite side of the sign-in/

sign-out sheet gave Ben a sense of authority. Maybe he could figure out how to sneak onto the computers and get Theo expelled.

"So this is life in administration," he said. His chin throbbed.

"Glamorous, isn't it?" said Mrs. Carlile, taking the kit from Wyatt. She pulled out an alcohol swab and Band-Aid. "It's just a scrape."

"Is there any blood on my shirt?" asked Ben. A person could only lose so many shirts in one week.

"Nope. Blood-free," she said.

Mrs. Carlile pressed an alcohol swab against Ben's chin. He winced, so she blew on the injury to take the sting away. Ben suddenly thought of his mother and wished he was home with her.

"First the Harry Potter ketchup blob, now this," Wyatt said. "Murphy's Law."

"Lunch is getting dangerous," said Ben. "Maybe I should hang out in here. Help around the office. Do whatever Wyatt does."

Wyatt yawned. "Yeah. We could use the help. We're swamped." He picked up a pen, clicked it three or four times, then put it down again. "If you can handle the excitement."

"Wyatt is a unique case," Mrs. Carlile said, positioning the Band-Aid over Ben's chin.

"Yep," Wyatt said. "That's me. Mr. Unique."

"I'm a unique case, too," said Ben. The Band-Aid was secure now, although it fit awkwardly. He tried to look Mrs. Carlile in the eye as she reorganized the first-aid kit. "I can't even walk without tripping over my own feet. It would be much safer for me in here." Ben looked around. "Maybe I can just help you out today."

Mrs. Carlile sighed thoughtfully. Ben raised his eyebrows. Her resolve was breaking; he could feel it.

"I guess it couldn't hurt," she said.

"Awesome," said Wyatt. "I'll give you a tour." He motioned to a cup full of pens. "These are the pens." Then he pointed to the copier. "That's the copier."

He took one step toward the sign-in/sign-out sheet. "There's the sign-out sheet. If someone needs to leave school early, they sign the sheet and then use that phone to call their parents. *They have to use the phone next to the sign-out sheet.* They can't use their cell phones. That's how we prevent truancy. Truancy means—"

"The action of staying out of school for no valid reason, also known as 'absenteeism,'" said Ben. The Band-Aid bunched when he talked.

"Yeah. Something like that." Wyatt pointed to Mrs. Carlile, who was sitting at her desk again. "And that's Mrs. Carlile and her desk. End of tour."

"That was fascinating," said Ben. "So what's our task at hand?"

"Basically we stand here until the bell rings. The main thing is we have to make sure kids who are leaving early sign out and use the right phone. It's pretty chill over lunch, though. So mostly I bother Mrs. Carlile with pointless questions until she tells me to shut up."

Ben glanced at Mrs. Carlile, who nodded at her monitor.

"What kind of questions?" asked Ben.

"For example," Wyatt said. "Why are you *in* a movie, but *on* TV?"

"Hmm. That's a good one."

"Why does pizza come in a square box instead of a round one?"

"Easier to stack, probably. Plus some people like square pizzas. And sometimes they put the extra sauce containers in the corners. And I bet it's easier to put together."

Wyatt raised a single eyebrow and nodded. "Interesting theories. How about this: Why is the third hand on a watch called the second hand?"

"He can do this forever," Mrs. Carlile said. "Look what you've started."

"I've got one," Ben said. "Why is it called a *ham*burger if it's made out of beef?"

Mrs. Carlile groaned.

Wyatt nodded proudly. "Awesome," he said.

They bumped fists.

Maybe I'll get tripped again tomorrow, Ben thought. *Then I'll never have to go to the lunchroom again.*

Questions

Rabbit Hole: *Starfish can interact with their environment, look for food, and respond to danger. They may appear to be insentient, but they can actually influence the world around them. There's more to starfish than meets the eye. Same with plant life.*

The dissection wouldn't require a scalpel, after all. They would use scissors instead. Miss Schneider held a pair up in front of the class with the image of a starfish projected behind her. Tomorrow was the day.

"You will use these to cut upward—away from yourself—toward the center of the sea star," she said.

"Then we'll view the pyloric ceca and parts of the endoskeleton, just under the skin. The sea star has five arms, as you know, so you and a lab partner will each have the opportunity to cut through at least one arm. You'll want to cut around the madreporite to expose the central disc area."

Lab partner.

Charlotte straightened and bent her knee, hoping to get rid of the throbbing pain there. Then she looked around the room. Magda was seated two desks behind Tori. She had her head down as she scribbled in her notebook. Her dark hair fell around her face. Charlotte whispered her name to get her attention, but she didn't look up. She whispered it a second time. When Magda caught her eye, Charlotte mouthed, "Lab partners?"

"Me?" Magda said quietly, pointing to herself. Confused.

Charlotte nodded and whispered, "Do you want to be lab partners?"

Tori's hand shot up as Magda nodded. "Miss

Schneider, can you repeat that last part?" She side-eyed Charlotte. "I was *distracted.*"

Charlotte fought the urge to roll her eyes.

"I was just discussing the characteristics that make sea stars unusual," Miss Schneider said. "Can anyone tell me where they fall in the evolutionary process? If you had to classify their appearance, would you say they are early in the process or late?"

"Late," said Tori, without waiting to be called on.

"Yes," said Miss Schneider. "Something else that's unusual about sea stars is their radial symmetry and the fact that they don't have heads or brains. At least, no brains to speak of. Question: Do you need a brain to be aware of your environment?"

Tori leaned toward Isabelle, who sat next to her, and tilted her head toward Charlotte.

"Starfish aren't the only things that can exist without brains," she whispered.

They laughed.

Charlotte raised her hand. Maybe because she knew

the answer. Maybe to muffle the laughing.

"They are aware of their environment," said Charlotte, quietly. "They have sensory structures and they're able to react to things around them, despite their reduced nervous system."

"Correct," Miss Schneider said. She put the scissors down. "Yes, Magda?"

Charlotte turned and looked at her new lab partner. Most of the other students did, too. Magda rarely raised her hand, even though everyone knew she was one of the smartest kids in school.

"Can they feel pain?" she asked.

Miss Schneider paused. "Sea stars have a central nervous system, so, yes. They can feel pain. But we aren't dissecting living specimens, so you don't have to worry about that."

Tori and Isabelle laughed again.

But Charlotte thought it was a good question.

She thought it was a very good question indeed.

Life According to Ben

Part XV

"If you make them laugh, they'll remember you forever," said Mr. Boxer.

Ben's father was home early for the first time this week. He was in the kitchen, making a pot of spaghetti. Mrs. Boxer was curled into a corner of the couch with a paperback. If you didn't know any better, you'd think it was just another Thursday night. But Ben knew better, so he planned to avoid the entire performance. "All the world's a stage." Shakespeare said that. Wait—was it Shakespeare or someone else?

Apparently, the stage at the Boxer house involved spaghetti.

Unfortunately, there are times when you have to get something from the kitchen and there's just no getting around it, no matter how fast you move. Ben didn't want to talk to his dad, but there was no way to get his water bottle from the refrigerator without crossing paths.

"So make sure you've got some good jokes in that speech," his father continued. He stopped stirring. "Do you need help? I can—"

"No thank you," Ben said quickly.

"What happened to your chin?"

"I fell. I already told Mom. Ask her."

Ben took a swig of water and headed back toward his room, navigating around his father's packed boxes along the way.

"Dinner will be ready soon."

"Don't want any!" Ben called over his shoulder.

Once he was inside his room of stasis, he locked the door and stared at it. He didn't have much experience with anger, but he was fairly certain that's what he felt now. He didn't really know where it was coming from, only that it was all directed toward his father. It was shooting off like sparks from a wand. He had no idea why his parents were splitting up, hadn't asked, didn't want to know, preferred not to talk about it; but something niggled inside his brain and told him it was his father's fault. His father was the one who complained the most. About work, mostly. But still.

It had to be somebody's fault—didn't it?

Confession

Rabbit Hole: *Stalagmites are formed from calcium salts that are deposited by dripping cave water. The drippings collect on a cave floor and grow taller and taller, sometimes reaching the top of the cave itself. Stalagmites grow slowly, collecting a drip at a time, and eventually become true wonders.*

"Confession," Ben Boot said. "I know four hundred words that start with the letter *Q*, and I don't know how to play basketball."

It was late. Charlotte was standing at her window, looking toward the Riveras' yard. Mateo was outside, stepping up on and down from a cinder block, one of his usual exercise routines. Charlotte used to get butterflies every time she saw him. But now when she looked into the backyard, she thought of Magda talking to her father over the stone wall. Him, pointing out the trees. Her, listening carefully.

"Well?" Ben said.

"Well what?"

"It's your turn to confess something."

"Okay." Charlotte walked to her dresser and picked through her rocks with her index finger. "I don't know how to play basketball, either."

"That doesn't count. You just repeated what I said."

"But it's true."

"Be that as it may."

Here's a confession: Sometimes Charlotte wished she could trade lives with someone else. When she was in the grocery store and saw someone laughing—one of those big laughs that lights up your whole face—she imagined walking up to that person and asking if they wanted to trade places. *Just for a little while,* she would say. And if they said no, she would go on: *Maybe we don't need to trade at all. I can just come with you. What's it like where you live? It must be nice if you can laugh like that.*

Here's another confession: Charlotte had a complete image of Lottie Lock, Scrabble champion. Lottie was pretty, smart, and funny. Lottie's parents were full of energy and life. They took her ice-skating. They went to amusement parks and the zoo. Lottie had hundreds of friends to choose from, too. They went to the shore in the summer and the Poconos in the winter. She never felt sad. She appreciated everything she had, but she didn't need much. Her bed was perfectly made every morning with the fluffiest, most comfortable pillows you could ever imagine. When she woke up, there were no tangles in her hair and she didn't have a crick in her neck. There were no clothes on the floor because she was perfectly tidy and organized. This girl—this perfect, perfect girl—never felt out of place because she was always in place. She knew what to say and was never scared. In her entire life, she would never hear *no wonder no one likes you.*

Lottie always had someone to sit with at lunch.

What was her middle name? *I should give her one,* Charlotte thought. *Melody, maybe.*

That reminded her of a time when she and Bridget had talked about what they'd name their future children.

"You always pick Melody," Bridget had said. She chose different names every time. Things like Chloe, Sadie, Sapphora, and Zane. "Pick something else."

"But I like Melody."

"It's just so . . . unoriginal."

So Charlotte picked something else. She didn't remember what. But she secretly stayed with Melody.

"Lottie?" said Ben. "Are you there?"

"Sorry," said Charlotte. "I zoned out."

She looked down at her hand and realized she was holding Sphinx. She didn't remember picking it up.

"What did you zone out about?"

Charlotte watched Mateo move on and off the cinder block. On any other day, she would have sent a text to Bridget: *Guess what I'm looking at right now?*

But this wasn't any other day.

"I was thinking about tomorrow," she said.

"Oh, yeah," said Ben. "Starfish dissection, right?"

That wasn't what Charlotte had been thinking about at all, actually. She was thinking about facing the morning bench alone again. She was wondering if she'd eat lunch on the roof. Would Bridget talk to her? But now she imagined the starfish, waiting for her and Magda to dissect it. She was thinking about how starfish feel pain. Even though she knew that tomorrow's specimens wouldn't feel anything—they were already dead, after all—she couldn't help but wonder if it would reach one of its arms toward the sky and ask *why, why, why*?

"Yeah," Lottie said. "But actually . . ."

She didn't know what she was about to say. The seeds of a plan grew in her mind. A dangerou ridiculous plan. But it felt like something differ Real.

Pick something real.

"Actually what?" Ben said.

"I was thinking of skipping."

Ben paused. "Skipping what?"

"School."

"Skipping *school*?" he repeated, as if she'd just said she planned to murder someone.

Charlotte's heart thumped in her chest.

"I'm going to spend my day at the art museum," she said, thinking about Gauguin. *Just wait until you see it, Charlotte*, her father had said. And she'd pretended to see, but she didn't really look. Instead, she'd asked to go home. "That's way better than anything we could ever learn at school, right? Besides, a starfish dissection is kinda gruesome, isn't it?"

She couldn't believe how casual she sounded. Oh, you know. Just another day of skipping school. I am Lottie Melody Lock, the girl who takes trains into Philadelphia. *C'est la vie.*

She placed Sphinx on her dresser and looked up train schedules while she talked.

"Haven't you ever skipped before?" she said.

"No. I've never missed a day of school in my life," said Ben. "Aren't you worried about getting caught?"

There was a train that left at 7:40 and got to Thirtieth Street Station at 8:20. According to MapQuest, the museum was a thirty-minute walk.

Could she walk that far?

Should she take a cab?

What was she even thinking?

Blood rushed to her ears.

Alone. In the city.

So what? It wasn't like she didn't have a plan. She would go to the museum, find Gauguin, Van Gogh, and whoever else, and head back to the station.

Nothing bad would happen.

It was easy. Simple, even. She just needed money for the train, the museum admission, and a cab, if she decided to take one. She'd been saving money to buy a coral fossil with botryoidal chalcedony stalagmites, but suddenly she didn't care.

How do you even hail cabs?

"Are you still there?" asked Ben.

"Yes," she said. She picked up Sphinx. "Sorry. I was looking at train schedules."

He paused. "I guess we both have big days tomorrow."

"Oh, that's right. Your speech." She clutched Sphinx so hard that it pressed into the soft flesh of her palm. "I have no doubt you'll kill it."

"I hope so," said Ben. "I want it to be the most memorable speech the student body has ever witnessed."

"I'm sure it will be."

Mateo wasn't there anymore.

Charlotte opened her window and felt a cool September breeze.

On the other end of the phone, she heard the vague sound of someone knocking on a door.

"That's my mom. She's probably going to force me to eat spaghetti," said Ben. "I better go."

"Okay," Charlotte said. "Listen, don't worry about tomorrow. You'll be amazing. I know it."

She hung up the phone.

She opened her window wider.

She reached her arm back.

And without a second thought, she tossed Sphinx as far as she could.

Life According to Ben

Part XVI

It wasn't his mom. It was his father.

"Can I come in?" he said.

Ben didn't want either of his parents to disrupt the stasis—his appropriately fluffed bed pillows, his smooth Ravenclaw comforter, the Star Wars Lego world he'd built three years ago and still kept in the corner. He didn't want devolving people in his land of sense and logic. But what can you say when your father asks to come into your room and his eyes are wide and sad looking? You say yes, even though you want to close the door and never come out.

Mr. Boxer sat at Ben's desk and faced his son, who leaned on the edge of the bed. Ben didn't want to sit and get comfortable because he didn't want to give the impression that this would be a long conversation.

"I know you're upset," his father said.

The smell of cooked pasta wafted through the open door. Ben secretly cursed his growling stomach. He didn't want to eat any of that tainted spaghetti, even if his father had added extra garlic and a dash of cinnamon, just the way he liked.

"You should talk about it," his father continued. "It'll make you feel better. You can ask us anything you want. You can ask *me* anything you want."

You're a chemist—don't you know about stasis? Why are you in here?

If you know how to correlate the properties of chemical substances to measure the effects of compounds and study interchemical reactions, you should be able to make a marriage work. Right? Smart people are supposed to do things the smart way, aren't they?

Where is your new apartment? Is it full of new furniture? Is there even a room for me?

Mom has all these new facial expressions that I don't understand. Do you recognize them?

How did all this happen without me even knowing? Did I not pay attention enough? Should I have?

Am I one of the reasons why you don't want to live here anymore?

Is it because I don't have enough friends and I'm always home when you are and you and Mom never have enough time to spend together?

"I," said Ben. He swallowed. "I don't have any questions."

Mr. Boxer nodded and looked at his feet. He was wearing white socks. He always wore white socks around the house and it drove Ben's mother crazy. She even bought him slippers one Christmas. But he only wore them on Christmas day.

Was that one of the reasons? Do people get divorced over slippers?

"You'll have questions eventually," Mr. Boxer said. "I won't push the issue. I just want you to know you can come to me or your mother." He paused. "I'm moving over the weekend. You can help out. Pick which room you want. Or even just come eat spaghetti tonight. We can still eat together as a family. Your mother and I are very amicable, Ben."

"There is evidence to the contrary," said Ben.

His father frowned and stood. "Well. If you want dinner, it'll be there for you."

After he left, Ben leaped from his bed so he could lock the door.

She Wondered

Rabbit Hole: *Lacrosse is French for "the stick." The earliest game was played by the Iroquois in the northeastern U.S. and could have originated as early as 1100 AD. In addition to the goalie and midfielders, lacrosse requires attackmen and defensemen.*

Charlotte couldn't sleep. She was in bed, still in her school clothes, thinking about tomorrow. She'd memorized the train schedule. She'd googled "how to hail a cab," and was relieved to learn that Thirtieth Street Station and the art museum usually had cabs parked outside. She knew the price of admission. She was ready. But her heart wouldn't stop thundering, and instead of getting a good night's rest, she lay awake, her mind wheeling and turning until she finally walked down the hall on the balls of her feet and went downstairs to the kitchen with her phone.

The pantry was stocked with heart-healthy snacks. She grabbed a bag of almonds, wished they were gummy bears, and had a sudden urge to fling the front door open and go screaming into the night, with nothing but almonds and the clothes on her back. How far would she get? Two blocks? Two miles? The next township? When would her feet start to hurt? What would it be like to leave everything behind?

Even if she ran for hours, it wouldn't matter. Her dad had a saying: *Wherever you go, there you are.* She'd once asked him what it meant and he said, "You can never run away from yourself." She was just a little kid at the time, and she pictured something out of Peter Pan—a shadow trying to escape its owner. But now she knew better.

Instead of fleeing out the front, she crept out the back. She'd never been in the backyard alone at this hour before. It was frightening and fantastic. The whole world was asleep and the stars were hers. She opened the almonds, lay down on the stone wall, and gazed up. The world was enormous, she was small, and so were all her problems.

If you don't see anything beautiful, change your viewpoint.

She shoved three almonds in her mouth, even though her mother always told her she should never eat lying down because she could choke to death. She wondered what it would be like to touch the stars and—just like that—they snapped on.

Only it wasn't the stars. It was the Riveras' back porch light.

Mateo came out, carrying a jump rope.

Who exercised at midnight?

Charlotte picked up her phone to text Bridget: *Guess who's jump-roping in the backyard right now?!*

But then she remembered, so she played a word instead.

SHINE.

She listened to the rope hit the patio. *Whoosh-plick, whoosh-plick, whoosh-plick, whoosh-plick.* She was superthirsty because of the almonds, but too self-conscious to move. He couldn't see her from his vantage point, but she didn't want to get up and go inside because then he might think she'd been spying on him.

Finally he went back inside, and that's when she got down from the wall and crossed the yard toward the back of her house. She was a few feet away from the back door when he emerged again with a water bottle.

"Hey," he said. Not *hey-how-are-you*, but *hey-I-have-something-to-ask-you*, which was unusual. Very unusual.

Charlotte stopped in her tracks.

Her throat was parched.

Mateo walked up to the edge of his yard. Charlotte turned toward him, but didn't move. She really didn't want him to see her puffy, red, and tired eyes.

"I want to ask you something," he said.

He was wearing a sweaty shirt that said PROVIDENCE HIGH SCHOOL LACROSSE.

Charlotte's heart stopped beating.

Her body was an enormous block of cement.

"Is it true that the kids at school make fun of my sister?"

Charlotte cleared her throat.

"What do you mean?" she asked, even though she already knew the answer.

"Like, calling her a freak. 'Mad Magda.' That kind of stuff."

Charlotte heard every cricket chirp in the dark, dark night. Were there crickets before? She could tell that Mateo was waiting for her to say something, but nothing came out of her mouth.

"She says the kids make fun of her sometimes," Mateo said.

Something plummeted in her chest. Like being

on a roller coaster and shooting straight down. She thought of Bridget holding the pear, glaring at Magda, and judging her—the uneven socks, faded shirt, weird habit of quoting poetry. Then Charlotte thought of the times she'd called her "Mad Magda" without a second thought. She had, hadn't she? Everyone did.

Charlotte had noticed the uneven socks and the faded T-shirt, too.

When had she started noticing those things?

"Some of the kids think she's weird," she said. She wanted to say that Magda had plenty of friends and that people never made fun of her at all. Instead, she told the truth. Mateo nodded and scanned the expanse of the yard. He had that look on his face, the one that used to make her and Bridget fake-swoon onto Charlotte's bedroom floor. It was that squinty-eyed look—the brooding secret he was dying to tell.

"One time my mom found this huge anthill in that corner," he said, pointing. "Magda accidentally stepped in it and had bites all over the place. We had to soak her feet in the bathtub and everything. My dad nearly busted his top. We have people take care of the lawn and he was superpissed that the anthill was there. The next day, my mom got this big thing of ant killer, like she was going into battle or something." He paused and faced Charlotte again. "When Magda saw it, do you know what she did?"

Charlotte shook her head.

"Started crying." Mateo laughed lightly. "She ran into the backyard and grabbed all these twigs and rocks and stuff. She said she was making one of those things—what do you call 'em? Those things that protect a village or whatever?"

"A fort?"

"Yeah, a fort. That's what it was. She was building a fort to save the ants from mom's ant killer. She said they didn't mean to attack her; they were just protecting themselves. She didn't want them to die. And they were just ants."

He pursed his lips and fidgeted with his bottle top.

"That's the kind of 'weird' she is," he said.

Charlotte couldn't speak. A huge bulb had lodged itself in the middle of her throat.

"I just thought someone should know," he said. He turned his back to her and set his water bottle on the patio table.

Charlotte didn't go back inside until he started jump-roping again.

Whoosh-plick.

FRIDAY

aberration *n* : an unwelcome departure from what is expected or, in astronomy, the displacement of an object from its true position

Life According to Ben

Part XVII

Ben was drinking a lot of water to keep his voice hydrated. He'd also kicked things up with his wardrobe. He wasn't just wearing a dress shirt; he was wearing the crisp blue suit that cost ninety-eight dollars at Macy's. His mother had bought it for his fifth-grade graduation. Unfortunately, it still fit.

It took Ben twenty minutes to decide which tie to wear. Blue or black? Blue or black? Blue or black? He alternated one with the other until he was dizzy and color-blind, but finally decided on blue. President Truman, considered one of the best-dressed presidents of the twentieth century, was fond of deep blues, and people considered him one of the greatest leaders of the modern age. The scab on Ben's chin was noticeable and dark, but the blue tie said: *Yeah, I have a scab, so what? You wanna make something of it?*

"Did you practice in front of the mirror last night?" his dad asked, when Ben emerged fully dressed from his bedroom on Friday morning.

Ben straightened his tie, even though it was already straight, and acted like he hadn't heard the question. He refilled his water bottle.

"Rehearsal is key. You want to memorize as much as you can," Mr. Boxer continued. He was rifling through the basket near the front door, where they kept the mail and the car keys. He snatched up the keys and jangled them in the air. "You need a ride to school?"

"Mom is taking me," Ben mumbled.

His back was turned to his father, so he couldn't

see the expression on his face. But it was probably a frown.

"Good luck today," Mr. Boxer said.

There was a pause before the front door opened and closed.

If Anyone Asks

Rabbit Hole: *About 143 million Americans commute to work each day. A study in 2013 showed that more than 70 percent of them didn't like their jobs. Studies also show that most people don't pursue their dreams. There are many reasons why, but one of them is lack of support or encouragement. Researchers at Ohio State University said any one person can often make a difference in another person's life, giving them the boost they need.*

Charlotte was usually awakened each morning by the sound of her mother hitting snooze and wandering half-dazed to the kitchen downstairs, but on Friday Charlotte woke up thirty minutes earlier than usual, dressed in the outfit she'd placed on her chair the night before, and left a note that she was going to school early with Bridget. She felt like a criminal when she stepped into the morning light. Her heart raced. Her throat tightened. She walked fast, fast, faster on her way to the station, certain that her mother would suddenly wake up and chase her down the street. But it was early and quiet. No mothers.

By the time Charlotte stood on the train platform, beads of sweat had collected on her hairline and neck. She looked at everyone around her—grown-ups cradling coffee, mostly—and felt like jumping out of her skin. Surely a twelve-year-old traveling alone would be suspicious, right? She had a cover story, of course. But she was sweating now, so did she look as nervous as she felt?

Should she embellish her story to explain her nervousness?

Count to ten, Charlotte.

Breathe in. Breathe out.

One, two, three, four . . .

It felt like a million eyes were on her, but no one was paying attention at all. They were on their cell phones. Sipping coffee. Edging toward the platform to crane their necks toward the tracks.

She was invisible.

She walked toward one of the benches all casual-like and sat down. No one else was sitting; they were too impatient for the train. She pretended she was playing a role in a movie. Casual twelve-year-old girl. Kind of like the role she had played in the library when Bridget called her a parasite.

She tapped her feet on the concrete.

This bench wasn't unlike the one at school. The one she shared with Bridget.

Or used to, anyway.

All the grown-ups looked bored and miserable.

I hope that's not how I look when I'm grown up.

Or do I look like that already?

She heard the train before she saw it. There was a slight rumble under her feet, and her heart tumbled out of her body and onto the tracks as it pulled up, screeching to a stop. Everyone huddled toward the sliding doors. They gravitated toward the same ones, even though several others opened at once. Charlotte wondered what she was supposed to do. Should she stand in the long line, or hurry to the open doors with no one waiting? Why did they all follow one another to the same doors when there were other open doors three cars away? Did they know something she didn't?

Charlotte took a few steps toward the doors down the tracks, but decided to turn back and stand in the line instead. She thought there must be a logical reason why no one wanted to go through the other doors until a girl with a Swarthmore College sweatshirt zipped in without a second thought. That's when Charlotte realized that the only reason people shifted toward these particular doors was because they all followed one another.

Like cattle, thought Charlotte.

Still, she stayed put. People were behind her now

and she was getting on the train already. She rubbed the back of her neck to wipe away some of the sweat, and then sauntered up to the line.

Was she really going to do to this?

Was her mother awake?

Was her mother in line behind her, ready to pull her back?

She slid into a seat and hoped no one sat next to her, but two stops later, a guy in a suit who reeked of cologne took the empty space. His cologne soaked into Charlotte's tongue. She leaned her head against the window, closed her mouth, and watched the Philadelphia suburbs tick by—Primos, Clifton, Gladstone.

She was breathless, but why? Was she scared? Elated? Nervous? Surprised? Anxious?

Maybe all of the above.

If anyone asked: She was going to see her dad in the city. Her parents recently got divorced, and her dad was in Philly for a work conference. This was the only day they'd be able to spend together, so she had to miss school. They were meeting at the art museum, then having lunch. Tonight he flew back to Cincinnati, so it was now or never.

Another suburb: Lansdowne.

The conductor came through the sliding door that connected the train cars. He snapped up pre-purchased tickets and made change.

"Fernwood, next stop!" he hollered.

He was big and burly. Charlotte pictured him leaning over scrawny Cologne Guy, narrowing his eyes at her, and growling: *What are you doing on this train by yourself, little girl?*

Her tongue and throat were dry as he made his way down the aisle. She wished she had water. She wished she was sitting next to a sweet grandmother. Then she could turn her body toward her and pretend they were together.

The conductor was closer.

The train rumbled.

Now he was at her seat. She barely heard anything except *whoosh-thump, whoosh-thump*—her heart.

Sweat beaded the back of her neck.

Cologne Guy flashed his ticket. The conductor looked at Charlotte. He was waiting for her to say something. Or he was about to pull her out of her seat by her hair and call the police. She didn't know which, so she sat there.

Get it together, Charlotte.

She suddenly had to pee.

The conductor stared at her. "Where to?" he said.

Open your mouth, idiot.

Speak.

Say it: Thirtieth Street Station.

Thirtieth Street Station.

"Where to?" he repeated. He looked completely annoyed now.

Cologne Guy side-glanced her way without picking up his head.

She sat up straight and handed the conductor her

money. "Thirtieth Street Station," she said.

She was amazed at how normal she sounded, like she did this every day. *Oh, sure. Thirtieth Street Station, if you please. I have business to attend to.*

The sweat evaporated. The heat in her cheeks disappeared.

She was Lottie Lock and she was going to Thirtieth Street Station. Any questions, mister?

Apparently not.

The conductor gave her a ticket and some change, and then moved on.

Life According to Ben

Part XVIII

Did President Grant's heart beat this loudly before a big speech? What about FDR? John Adams?

Ben liked to think the answer was yes.

The boys' bathroom wasn't exactly the ideal place to prep for the biggest speech of your life. Eisenhower and Ford probably didn't have bright pink soap in half-broken dispensers hanging from the walls while they prepared to address Congress, but this was the best Lanester Middle School had to offer. There was an hour before speech time, and Ben hadn't been able to calm down. Sure, he looked like a normal kid breezing down the hall, but he was a jumble of nerves inside. Every part of him trembled. He'd never had this problem before. He was no stranger to the spotlight. He'd received awards in front of crowds, competed in academic championships, won best cosplay at the Potter Festival in Houston two years ago. But this was different. He paced in front of the urinals and thought: How did I get into this? Why did I do this? How did this start? He thought of how far behind he was. Only four days into the race and he was already giving a speech. He secretly resented Mrs. Carlile for letting him register late. Why did she have to do that? Why couldn't she just follow the rules?

Who was he kidding, anyway?

He didn't even have anyone to sit with at lunch. Who would vote for him?

He stopped pacing and stared at himself in the mirror.

"Stop the negative self-talk," he said to himself. "You can do this."

He shook out his hands and rolled his neck back and forth.

"You just need to relax," he said.

He knew his speech front-to-back. It was a good speech. On the level of the Gettysburg Address, as far as middle-school speeches went. If he lost this thing, he would lose with dignity. He would go out big. People would remember Ben Boxer after this.

"You don't need to win the election," he whispered. "You just need to win this speech. It will still be a victory. It will still be evolution."

You are a finch.

You are a finch.

When the door to the bathroom opened, he pretended he'd been washing his hands. Two boys walked in—guys he'd never seen before. They snickered at his suit.

"You going to church or something?" one of them said.

"Saint Urinal!" said the other.

Ben dried his hands and left. He didn't have time for them. He had a speech to conquer and a larynx to hydrate.

He made a beeline for the water fountain, refilled his bottle, and took a deep, deep breath.

Yes, Ben Boxer. You are a finch.

Only

Rabbit Hole: *There's a 43-foot complete fossil specimen of a dinosaur at the Academy of Natural Sciences in Philadelphia. Independence Hall welcomes more than 690,000 visits per year. At the Franklin Institute, children can walk through a giant heart.*

Charlotte had gone into the city with her parents before, but she didn't remember it being this crowded. When the train pulled into the station, people moved like one massive beast and they took her along with them. She could be swallowed whole and spit out, but there was something exhilarating about it, too. Like she was one of them. An adult going to work. Maybe she was a curator at the Academy of Natural Sciences, a tour guide at Independence Hall, or director of the Franklin Institute. *Out of the way, people. I have an early meeting.*

She kept her eyes straight ahead and walked down the platform like she knew what she was doing. Her heart squeezed as she went past the panhandlers. It plummeted when she breezed by a police officer. But it lifted again as she entered the station itself, that big cavernous building that looked like something out of an old movie.

When she stepped outside, a gust of wind slapped her in the face. This was the part where she was supposed to get into a cab and here they were, parked and waiting. She hesitated.

Breathe, Charlotte. In. Out.

Was this the part where she would get busted? She imagined the driver taking one look at her and saying, *Why aren't you in school?* and driving her straight to the police station. Instead, he asked, "Where to?" without a second glance.

"Philadelphia Museum of Art, please," Charlotte said.

Was it okay to say please? Did that make her seem like less of a city girl?

The driver didn't seem to notice. He pulled out of the station and she was Lottie Lock. Someone who took cabs and navigated through big cities. A character in a movie who knew secrets and important people. A girl who had it all together.

Only.

There was still sweat on her neck and even though she didn't want to admit it—especially not to herself—she was having second thoughts. She was like one of those drawings in the puzzle books she had loved in elementary school. *Something in this picture doesn't belong. What is it? Answer on page 100. And the answer is Charlotte Lockard.*

Life According to Ben

Part XIX

It would have been a great speech.

They would have cheered.

They would have stood.

They would have pumped their fists in the air and chanted his name.

His speech would have boomed through the microphone and filled the gym with confidence and hope for a brighter Lanester Middle School. His voice would have drowned the smell of dirty sneakers and basketballs and given rise to a new era: the administration of Ben Boxer.

They would have realized how wrong they were. How they misjudged him.

That day, before the speech, he'd walked the halls and discovered that some of his posters had been ripped down the middle. They dangled off the wall hopelessly, like deflated balloons. But he didn't let that sway him. No: At that point, he still had a speech to give. He still had an opportunity to win them over. They would soon realize how foolish they'd been to dismiss his brand and his ideas, he'd thought.

At that point, his suit was still starched and crisp.

But that was then.

Now his pants and jacket were shoved in the plastic bag next to his chair in the attendance office, where he slumped in the oversized gym shorts Mrs. Carlile pulled from some god-awful lost-items drawer. The shorts smelled like feet and he had to hold them bunched in one hand so they wouldn't fall to his ankles. To make matters worse, he was wearing his polished dress shoes. No socks. His socks were in the plastic bag, too.

He leaned his head on his hand and imagined how it would have been.

They would have fidgeted in their seats before coming to attention—all eyes on him. He would have been John F. Kennedy. Ask not what your country can do for you. Abraham Lincoln. A house divided against itself cannot stand. FDR. The only thing we have to fear is fear itself.

"Your mom is on her way to sign you out," Mrs. Carlile said. "Do you need anything?"

He didn't want to look at her because he knew her face was lined with pity, and he didn't want pity now. He wanted to crawl into the soft comfort of his bed, throw the covers over his head, and disappear. It was a strange feeling. He'd never wanted to disappear before. He'd always wanted to stand out.

I guess you got your wish, he thought.

He tried to shake his head, but he had no energy for interaction, so he didn't respond. He listened to the imaginary roar of the crowd. In his imaginings, they laughed at his joke, the one he'd practiced again and again (pause for laughter, his notes said).

When his mom showed up, he was still sitting in the same position. Her eyebrows furrowed at the sight of him. He sensed her confusion. *What's wrong with my perfect pineapple?*

"Ben?" she said.

He didn't move. If he moved, everything would be real. And he didn't want anything to be real. He wanted to push himself into the wall and become part of the building.

"The principal would like to speak to both of you before you go," said Mrs. Carlile to his mother. "I'll walk you over."

She and Ben's mother made their way toward the main office.

What goes on there that doesn't happen here?

I guess you're about to find out, Ben Boxer.

Mr. Finch.

Straight Ahead

Rabbit Hole: *Art has been proven to improve emotional well-being. It can also spark innovation and provide healing. Art is a fundamental component of a healthy community.*

Art was supposed to make you feel something. That's what her dad always said.

"It's in our lives every day, if you look for it," he'd say, pointing at a crack in the sidewalk, a spray of graffiti, or a drift of wildflowers sprouting in a parking lot. It had irritated Charlotte, the way he thought everything had deeper meaning. Wildflowers were wildflowers. Graffiti was graffiti. And that crack in the sidewalk? Tree roots pushing their way up, making room for themselves.

Her mother said he was "overly romantic" in how he approached the world. Charlotte's mother buried herself in numbers, research, and facts. When Charlotte asked how they ever got along, her mother said, "Someone has to be looking straight ahead instead of at the clouds."

Maybe her father was right. But as Charlotte walked up the massive steps of the art museum, she only felt small.

She understood chlorophyll and isotopes and erosion. She understood that sedimentary rocks were formed by the deposition and cementation of material at the earth's surface. When she stood in front of Van Gogh and Gauguin, she just saw paint on canvas. Not that interesting. No science. Nothing she could slide under a microscope or pull from the earth.

She should have paid more attention when her father talked.

Played more Scrabble.

Walked into the room.

Life According to Ben

Part XX

"You could have sworn a gun went off, but it turned out to be bang snaps," said Mrs. Yang, the principal. She was a kind-faced woman. If Ben was feeling more like himself, he would ask about the photos on her bookshelf and the accolades on her wall, but instead he sat and stared at a nick in her desk that reminded him of the dark mark from Harry Potter. Seemed fitting.

Mrs. Carlile sat to his left, his mother to his right. All eyes on him.

Mrs. Yang frowned. "They threw them just as Ben started his speech. They were sitting in the front row on the bleachers, right in front of the podium."

"Who are 'they'?" asked Mrs. Boxer.

"Theo Barrett, Derrick Vass, and David Landry," said Mrs. Yang.

"Sherry Bertrand, too," Mrs. Carlile added. "Bunch of little tyrants."

"It could have been complete chaos, what with the popping sounds and everything. A few kids screamed, but not everyone heard it, and Ms. Abellard took action right away. She realized they were just firecrackers and really averted what could have been a disaster."

Just firecrackers, Ben thought. The word *just* dug into his skin.

"I don't understand," Ben's mother said.

Ben simultaneously wanted to hug his mother and tape her mouth shut.

He slunk down in his chair and kept his eyes focused on the dark mark. He decided to think of something else. Was Mrs. Yang's desk oak or pine? How do you tell the difference? Maybe it was cherrywood. . . .

"They threw the bang snaps just as Ben was getting started," Mrs. Yang said. Her voice was hesitant, like she wanted the words to land as softly as possible.

"Did they interrupt the other kids' speeches, too?" his mother asked.

There was a pause. A long, giant, heavy pause.

"No," Mrs. Yang said. "Just Ben's."

Ben heard his mother exhale.

"It terrified several of the students." Mrs. Yang paused. "And I'm sure Ben was already nervous, giving a speech in front of the school and all."

The air choked him.

Mrs. Carlile leaned over and put a hand on Ben's shoulder. It felt like hot coal. He wanted to shake it off.

"We immediately hauled them to the office," Mrs. Yang continued. "One of our teachers noticed something was wrong with Ben, so she walked over, made a very nice announcement that all the speeches would be postponed." Mrs. Yang picked up a pencil, put it down again. "She got him out of there. I don't think anyone noticed anything out of place."

Not true, Ben thought. People noticed. He'd heard them laughing, snickering. All it would have taken was one person to see. Ms. Abellard had done her best to block their view, but there's only so much you can do.

Just one person. That's all it takes.

"Students of Lanester Middle School—" That's all he'd been able to say.

He didn't think he'd ever talk again.

His beak had been stitched together.

Silence swelled inside the office—an uncomfortable nothingness that radiated toward Ben and threatened to suffocate him, until it was broken by a faint but distinct buzz.

It was his phone, which was in his pants, which were in the plastic bag at his feet. When Ben didn't move, Mrs. Carlile rummaged around, looking for it. He felt faintly sorry that she had to stick her hand in his damp clothes to stop the buzzing, all while he sat there. But he was incapable of moving.

"It's a Pennsylvania number," she said, softly.

You weren't supposed to have cell phones at school. If you did, they had to be turned off and stowed away. Ben never bothered with that because no one ever called or texted him during the day anyway. He wondered if he would get a reprimand. *Ben Boxer, I realize you are the biggest dork in school and now the district's—no, the state's—greatest laughingstock, but phones are not allowed.*

The phone stopped buzzing. There was a pause. Then it buzzed again. It wasn't Lottie's number.

He didn't want to talk to anyone. He wanted to become part of the carpet or Mrs. Yang's desk. But Lottie Lock had skipped school today. She was taking the train into the city.

"There's a text," said Mrs. Carlile. "It says it's an emergency."

The word *emergency* replaced the uncomfortable silence in the room with anxious static.

The phone buzzed again.

"Do you know anyone in Pennsylvania?" his mother asked.

"Yes," Ben said.

He took the phone and answered it.

Soldier at Attention

Rabbit Hole: *Sunflowers are the subject of two series of still life paintings by the Dutch painter Vincent van Gogh. The earlier series (painted in 1887) shows flowers lying on the ground. The second series (from 1888) shows bouquets of sunflowers in a vase.*

Charlotte was standing in front of the sunflowers again.

She had visited Gauguin, seen Degas, and squinted at dozens of portraits and sculptures. She stood in front of them with her hands behind her back, just like her dad did. For some reason—she wasn't sure why—she kept coming back to Van Gogh.

She looked as hard as she could.

She tilted her head to the left.

She tilted her head to the right.

She saw a painting of sunflowers. Paint on canvas. That was it.

The gallery was quiet except for a few older couples who moved from painting to painting with their hands behind their backs and a man in a jacket who kept an eye on everyone.

Charlotte took a step closer.

Vase with Twelve Sunflowers.

That was the name of the painting, and that's exactly what she saw.

She took another step and leaned forward.

"You have to keep a distance of at least one foot between you and the work," said the man in the jacket, who was suddenly standing next to her.

She stood up straight, like a soldier at attention. "Oh."

He hovered near her as if she were a criminal, and

now she was too self-conscious to keep looking at the painting. The whole trip was a mistake. The scab on her knee ached after climbing all the museum stairs and it felt wrong being out of school. She wasn't a new person at all. She wasn't Lottie Lock or a character in a movie. She was the girl from the puzzle who didn't fit in the picture.

Who didn't fit anywhere.

She didn't know who she was.

Plus, she was hungry. She'd forgotten about lunch.

"You keep coming back to that painting," the man in the jacket said. He reminded her of her father, only he was older. Her father had deep brown eyes and a long face. Not like this man, whose name tag said JOSEPH. But there was something about him. Or maybe there wasn't.

"I was trying to . . . ," Charlotte began. "I was waiting to feel something."

It seemed like a ridiculous thing to say, but Joseph nodded like he knew exactly what she was talking about.

"But I just see sunflowers," Charlotte said.

"Well, that's what they are," said Joseph.

The truth was, she *did* feel something. She felt like she should have invited her father to Red's. She felt like she should have gone to school so Magda wouldn't have to dissect the starfish alone.

"Some people see things just as they are," said Joseph. "Nothing wrong with that."

"But how do—" Charlotte stopped. She heard the determined *click-click-click* of shoes against the museum floor. The walk of someone with a purpose.

Her mother.

Charlotte was suddenly hollow. Exposed. Stupid. Scared. And she couldn't read the expression on her mother's face. She'd never seen it before. She'd never seen her mother walk so quickly. The sound of her shoes bounced off the walls.

Charlotte opened her mouth, but her voice had disappeared. Her throat was a knot.

My father's dead.

Her mother's eyes were rimmed, glistening, and pink.

That's why she's crying.

"What are you doing here?" her mother said. She grabbed Charlotte and hugged her. She spoke into Charlotte's shoulder. "What are you doing?"

Charlotte sputtered, "I wanted . . . I thought . . ." then hugged her mom back and said, "I don't know."

"You scared me to death." Her voice was muffled against Charlotte's shirt.

Was she crying?

Her mother never cried. There could only be one reason.

"Is Dad dead?" Charlotte asked. She hadn't meant the words to sound so definite, so raw. But if he was dead, she needed to know now.

Her mother let her go. Her eyes glistened. "No. Oh no. That's— He's in his new room. He's asking for you."

"He is?"

"Of course." She sniffled. "That's why I went to your school. To sign you out. And they said—"

Charlotte imagined them telling her that she was absent. Her mother's confused expression.

The tears were for her, not her father.

"—they said you weren't there," she continued. "That you never got to school at all. I was so confused." She took a deep breath. "I asked Bridget, and she said she hadn't talked to you. Didn't know anything about it."

"You talked to Bridget?"

But then Charlotte remembered the note.

Her mother nodded. "Then I pulled up your phone records. I was in a total panic. So many things happen to kids—" She glanced at Joseph as if to say: *You're a grown-up. You understand, right?* He nodded. "—I saw all these Louisiana numbers and I thought you ran off with some maniac from the internet."

The thought of Ben being a maniac from the internet made Charlotte smile, even though it wasn't the best time to be smiling—or maybe it was, because now her mother was smiling, too. She looked around, as if she just realized where they were.

"Why did you come here, of all places?" her mother asked.

"I was just . . . ," Charlotte began. "I was . . ."

I just wanted to feel something.

Her mother grabbed her hand and squeezed.

"Let's just go now, okay? Let's go and see your father."

Life According to Ben

Part XXI

Humiliation was exhausting, but it had lulled him into a deep, deep sleep—so deep that his head pounded when he woke up and his mouth felt like parchment. He was in the same spot where he'd collapsed and his first thought was that he needed a glass of water, but then he thought of all the water he drank before the speech and . . . he pushed that thought away. He stretched. He blinked his eyes.

He felt strange. He'd never been onc for naps, even

though more than 85 percent of mammalian species were polyphasic species that slept for short periods throughout the day. He needed a nice warm shower and a nice new life. But he decided to roll over and go back to sleep instead.

Before he could, there was a knock on the door and it opened.

He'd forgotten to lock it.

Groan.

"Ben." It was his father. Fantastic. What was he doing here, anyway? What time was it? Did he leave work to rush over and comfort his disappointment of a son?

The bed shifted as his father sat down.

"You know . . . ," his father began. "There's this saying by Robert Frost. It goes, 'In three words I can sum up everything I know about life: It goes on.'"

Great, thought Ben. *All my problems are solved.*

"Sometimes things happen to people who don't deserve it," his father continued. "Sometimes other people do stupid things and it winds up affecting people around them, and it feels really unfair." Pause. "Do you know why it feels unfair?"

Ben didn't say anything. His father's voice was heavy and strange in the space around them. Stasis had been disrupted.

What was the opposite of stasis?

"Because it is," his father answered. Pause. "Franklin Roosevelt had polio, you know."

He was really pulling at straws now, wasn't he?

"Duh," said Ben. He was talking into his pillow because he didn't want to lift his head, so he couldn't see the expression on his father's face. He didn't care, anyway. "*Everyone* knows that."

He'd never snapped at either of his parents before, but he was angry and sad and humiliated and lonely, and it had to go somewhere.

"True. Most people do," continued his father. "But did you know that he fought his paralysis every step of the way? He tried all the therapies that were available to him. He even founded hydrotherapy centers for the treatment of polio. He founded the March of Dimes, too."

Ben closed his eyes. *Leave me alone. I just want to go to sleep.*

But his dad kept talking.

"Roosevelt wasn't just smart. He was resilient." The bed lifted back in place as Mr. Boxer stood and walked toward the door. "I bet he was a Ravenclaw."

Ben didn't move.

He wanted to sleep forever.

He wanted to imagine he was someone else.

He wanted to keep being mad at his father, because he had to be mad at someone.

But then he opened his eyes.

"By the way," Mr. Boxer said, as he opened the bedroom door. "Who's this girl, Charlotte?"

Ben lifted his head, and turned to his father.

"The person I'm going to call when I win the lottery," he said.

Hemlock

Rabbit Hole: *Socrates was given hemlock in his tea. This was a common way to poison condemned prisoners in ancient Greece. Allegedly, his last words were: "We owe a rooster to Asclepius. Don't forget to pay the debt."*

The room smelled like flowers. Charlotte hadn't expected that. Her father's friends and old colleagues had sent them. They were perched on the windowsill and the bedside table. She thought it would smell like medicine, like the bottles Ms. Schneider used for experiments. She thought she would hear beeping, like on TV. *Beep. Beep. Beep.* But everything was quiet.

Her father was asleep. Charlotte sat down in the chair next to the bed. The seat was worn and warm. A stack of magazines towered on the floor next to it. *Atlantic Monthly, Smithsonian, Harper's.* Her mother's.

She didn't want to wake her father, so she studied the folds in the blanket. The way the wires from the IV dangled from his hand. He didn't look as sickly as she feared he would. In fact, he didn't look sick at all. Just asleep.

Had his hair always been so white?

Yes, as long as Charlotte could remember. Her mother had told her a million times that his hair had once been a soft blond. Strawberry blond. By the time Charlotte was in elementary school, most of it had turned white.

Charlotte wondered if her hair would ever turn white. It was hard to imagine.

"Hey," her father said, blinking. He yawned. "Fancy seeing you here."

"Mom is getting coffee," Charlotte said. She wanted

to explain why she hadn't been in sooner; instead, she held up a leaf she'd plucked from the sidewalk on her way in.

"Look," she said.

He rubbed his eyes, slipped on his reading glasses, and tilted his head back to study it.

"Eastern hemlock," he said.

Charlotte hesitated. Her fingers suddenly burned. "Isn't that what killed Socrates? Hemlock?" she finally said.

She'd fallen into a rabbit hole once. Cleopatra to Socrates, somehow. Then Socrates to hemlock. Hemlock could kill in even small doses. Its toxins blocked the neuromuscular function, causing paralysis of the respiratory muscles. She flexed her hands. Had it seeped through her skin? Was it seeping through her father's?

"No," he said. "Well, yes—hemlock killed Socrates. But not this hemlock. This hemlock is perfectly safe. It's the official state tree of Pennsylvania. You can even put it in your tea." He twirled it in his fingers.

"How was the starfish? That was today, wasn't it?"

"Oh," said Charlotte. She thought of Magda without a lab partner and frowned. "Technically, yes. But I didn't go to school today."

He raised his eyebrows. "You didn't? I thought your mom went to sign you out."

"I kind of . . . skipped, I guess."

"You?"

"Yeah. It was dumb."

"Where did you go? What could possibly be more riveting than middle school?"

Charlotte bit her bottom lip. She remembered the terrified look on her mother's face and the warmth of her arms around her.

"I went to the art museum," she said. "To look at the Post-Impressionists."

For a moment, her father didn't say anything. Then he released a loud and hearty laugh. Eventually he stopped, clutching his chest, saying that he was still a little sore, but it was worth it.

"And what did you think?" he asked.

"Honestly?"

He nodded.

"Looked like a bunch of paint on a canvas."

He laughed again. "You're just like your mother."

Under normal circumstances, this would have bothered her.

It would have made her skin crawl.

She would have protested.

But these weren't normal circumstances.

S A T U R D A Y

reciprocal *adj* : a mutual relationship—one that is equal, matching, and complementary

Life According to Ben

Part XXII

Ben wasn't sure what it was supposed to feel like to have a second bedroom in a new place. He tried to analyze his emotions and determine if they were the right ones, but this was a different world.

His parents were getting divorced.

This upset him greatly.

But he couldn't help it: He liked his room in his father's apartment and all the fresh boxes with new and disassembled bookshelves. He liked the idea of having a second place, even if he was the same Ben.

Was this evolution?

He carried the last of the boxes inside and set them next to his skeletal bed frame. Later, they would pick out a mattress. His father didn't know it yet, but Ben planned to pick the best Sleepwell mattress they could find. According to the commercials and his internet research on *Consumer Reports*, Sleepwell was the ideal mattress. It conformed to the body's natural shape. It was also unusually expensive, which normally would have made Ben hesitant and guilt-ridden, but he felt slightly justified, since he wasn't the one who asked to have two rooms in the first place.

He lived in a world of logical things, and he considered this quite logical. After all, some things aren't fair. His dad said so himself.

He stood in the center of his boxes and turned in a circle to look at all the blank walls. He wondered how he would decorate his room. Everything smelled like fresh paint and carpet.

The complex had a swimming pool, which was another plus.

His father unpacked boxes in a nearby room. He'd plugged in an ancient radio—he called it a "boom box"—and played old rock music, but he didn't sing along, which was a definite plus.

"Maybe I'll choose something more academic for this room," Ben said, aloud.

Maps? He loved maps.

He wondered what other kids put on their walls.

Probably not maps.

Another bonus: His window faced the sidewalk, which was nicely shaded by magnolia trees. Natural light was better for neural synapses. He pulled back the curtain. The scent of the fabric pierced his nose. Everything here was fresh out of the box.

He stared at the sidewalk, trying to imagine his new life as Apartment-Complex Ben. He was still in the same school district, and it wasn't far from home, so he'd been through this neighborhood before. But it might as well be Mars now.

A kid was making his way up the sidewalk on foot. Ben craned his neck.

Someone familiar.

He pushed the window up. The humidity of south Louisiana immediately rushed inside.

"Hey!" Ben called out. "Wyatt!"

Wyatt looked around, startled, until he finally spotted Ben through the screen. He hesitated and squinted.

Ben's confidence nose-dived. He'd been so excited to see Wyatt that he'd forgotten about his social status, which had gone from nonexistent to pariah. He knew how middle school worked. Some people were liabilities. You don't want to be seen with the kid who . . .

The kid who was Ben Boxer.

"Life goes on," his father had said.

I hope it hurries up, Ben thought.

"Hey," said Wyatt. He walked across the grass to

the window. "I didn't know you lived here."

"I don't," said Ben. "Well, I do. As of today." He pointed a thumb over his shoulder. "I'm helping my dad move in and I guess I'll be here on the weekends or whatever."

"I live here, too," Wyatt said. "Building A."

"I'm in Building F," said Ben, as if Wyatt wasn't standing right in front of it.

"Cool. There's a pool here and everything, you know."

"Cool," Ben said. He didn't usually say "cool," but it seemed to fit.

Wyatt cleared his throat. "Sorry about the speeches, man. Theo and those guys are brainless idiots."

"Yeah," said Ben. His cheeks burned.

"Good news is, they got in a ton of trouble. So that's something."

"Yeah. It's something."

"It sucks that you have a blemish on your perfect record now. You have officially missed one half-day of school. As an ambassador of the attendance office, I'm sorely disappointed."

"Well . . . ," said Ben, laughing nervously. "I think I'm done with public life for a while. No more running for any offices."

Wyatt lifted a finger. "Question. Why do they call it 'running' for office? I mean, you're not actually running."

"And why do cars and trucks carry shipments, but ships carry cargo?" Ben offered.

Wyatt tapped his chin. "Good point. Good point." He stuffed his hands in his pockets. "Well. It's been fun talking to you through this screen and everything, but I'm on my way to get a Footlong Coney from Sonic."

"Footlong Coney?"

Wyatt blinked then dropped his mouth open in mock surprise. "You've never had a Footlong Coney?"

"I've never been to Sonic."

"You've never been to Sonic?"

"My parents aren't crazy about fast food."

Wyatt shook his head. "What a terrible upbringing you've suffered." He waved his hand in the direction he'd been walking as if to say "come with." "I can't let this injustice go any further. Injustice is an enemy of all good things."

"I agree," said Ben.

He shut the window, rushed into the living room to get money from his dad, then stepped into the warm afternoon.

Just Like the Sky

Rabbit Hole: *Researchers have studied the science of friendship and found that having a healthy and reciprocal relationship with a friend can alleviate emotional pain and improve physical health. One of the most important aspects of a healthy relationship is an equal amount of give-and-take.*

The sky changed colors above Charlotte's head. The shift from afternoon to evening. She was lying on the stone wall with her knees up. When her phone buzzed, she assumed it was Ben. But it wasn't.

"Hey," said Bridget. "I haven't seen you in a few days."

It's weird, with best friends. They share a certain kind of energy, a knowingness. You can finish each other's sentences. You can read each other's thoughts. And even though Bridget had only uttered one sentence, Charlotte knew this was the beginning of an end. The seasons were changing, just like the sky. Just like the leaves. They thought they'd be best friends forever, but sometimes forever isn't what you expected. Sometimes life is unfair. Unexpected.

But sometimes it brought its surprises. Like Ben Boot, who she now knew was Ben Boxer. That morning he'd played DAWN.

"I was just calling to see how your dad was doing," said Bridget.

Her voice was the same, but it felt like years since they'd spoken, even though it'd only been a few days.

Time was strange that way.

Parasite, Bridget had said.

But during the hour or so that Charlotte had been on the wall, picking apart the week and rolling things over in her mind, she'd decided something: She didn't care.

Well, that wasn't totally true.

She cared.

But she wouldn't always.

"He's fine," said Charlotte. "He's coming home soon."

"That's great."

"Yeah."

There was a time when no silence existed between them, when it would be filled with giggles or gossip or nonsense or deep and meaningful questions. But they had been two different people.

When had that happened?

Maybe I would have noticed if I'd paid better attention, Charlotte thought.

Or maybe it's subtle. Something you can barely feel. Like a slow slip.

"Well, I better go," said Bridget, breaking the silence. "Sophie and I are going to the movies." She paused. "Do you wanna come with us?"

"Nah."

Charlotte heard the Riveras' back door open.

Was it Mateo?

"Have fun, Bridget," Charlotte said. "Tell Sophie I said hi."

She hung up and stared at DAWN. She added -ING. It was the best she could do, but it worked.

DAWNING.

She sat up and stretched. For the first time in her life, she was relieved to see Magda instead of Mateo.

"Hey," said Magda. She walked across the yard, holding something in her hand.

"Hey," Charlotte dangled one leg off the side of the wall. "I'm really sorry about yesterday."

"Why? What happened yesterday?"

"The dissection. I was supposed to be your lab partner."

"Don't worry about it," she said. "I got paired up with Val Paretti. She's nice, but she didn't want to cut any of the arms, so she let me do it. Double win." She opened her fist. "I found something in my yard and I thought you might like it."

Charlotte recognized it immediately.

"That's Sphinx," Charlotte said. She swung both legs over and hopped down. It didn't even occur to her that she was standing in Mateo's yard for the first time.

She took it from Magda's hand. "This is my Egyptian quartz. I threw it out the window the other day. I'm so glad you found it."

They both hovered over it, their hair falling around their faces.

"Why did you throw it out the window?" Magda asked.

"I don't know. I was mad, I guess."

"You don't seem like the type who would throw something. Then again, my dad doesn't seem like the type who would watch reality television, and it's all he ever does when he's not at work. The greatest mystery of people isn't learning what they are, but learning what they aren't."

"Which poet said that?"

"Magda Rivera." She poked Sphinx with her finger. "You should really consider throwing something else instead next time. Like, a sock or something."

Charlotte lifted her head and put Sphinx in her pocket.

"Hey," she said. "Do you wanna come over and play Scrabble?"

"Sure."

When Charlotte pulled the board from the closet, dust misted down with it. But not as much as she expected. She carried it to the dining room table, Magda at her heels.

"Are you any good?" Magda asked, sitting in the chair underneath the pear.

"I'm currently number two on the online leaderboard," Charlotte said, setting up the game board. "But playing online is a lot different than playing face-to-face."

"I can't remember the last time I played a board

game." Magda pulled a rack toward her and shook the bag of letters. *Rattle. Rattle. Rattle.*

"It's a lost art," Charlotte said. She sat down, too.

The grid stretched between them.

Technically, players were supposed to pull tiles from the bag and whoever got the earliest letter from the alphabet started the game.

But today Charlotte motioned toward the bag and smiled. She felt lighter, somehow.

"You go first," she said.

A Sneak Peek at

Erin Entrada Kelly's *Lalani of the Distant Sea*

"A lush and mysterious fable,
full of beauty, full of wonder."
—Rebecca Stead, Newbery Medal-winning
author of *When You Reach Me*

Lalani of the Distant Sea

WINNER OF THE NEWBERY MEDAL FOR *HELLO, UNIVERSE*

ERIN ENTRADA KELLY

There are stories of extraordinary children who are chosen from birth to complete great quests and conquer evil villains.

This is no such story.

Sometimes, you are an ordinary child.

Sometimes, you choose yourself.

Come closer. Nestle deep. Travel now to two mountains. They are alive, at least to those who live among them. One of them towers darkly. It casts a shadow of vengeance, impatience, and fear. The Sanlagitans call it Mount Kahna.

The other mountain—if you can call it that—is bathed in light. Set foot here, and you will have all of life's good fortunes, whatever those may be. This is Mount Isa.

You can't see Isa now. No human has ever laid eyes on her. Nevertheless, the Sanlagitans are certain the mountain calls to them. They die trying to answer. They attempt journey after journey. They are pushed by their faith, not knowing that they believe in the wrong things.

Their ships sink. Their souls break. And yet, they make the trip, because they feel Isa's presence on an invisible horizon. Somewhere far away, yet close enough to touch. Somewhere beyond the distant sea.

The Three of Them

Twelve-year-old Lalani Sarita had heard the story of the mountain beast many times. She knew of his mangled face, his house of stolen treasures, and his penchant for evil trickery, but she begged to hear it all again anyway. It was the perfect night for ghost stories. The moon cast a bluish glow through the slats of the Yuzi house, and jars of bulb flies shined like stars in the corners of the front room. Lo Yuzi leaned forward in her rocking chair to eye the members of her audience closely. There were three of them, of course: Lalani; her best friend, Veyda; and Veyda's younger brother, Hetsbi.

"Imagine you are an old man," Lo Yuzi, who was Veyda and Hetsbi's mother, said. She spoke in the loudest of whispers, and the chair creaked when she moved. Her hands, rough and scarred from years of pulling plants, sat folded on her lap. "Your face is weary with wrinkles, and your nose is missing."

Lalani pressed her palms to her cheeks and pulled them down, imagining her face sagging with age. Hetsbi, who was only one year younger than the girls, laughed behind a closed fist.

"You live alone on Mount Kahna," Lo Yuzi continued. "You spend your days all alone, dreaming of your other life, when you had friends and family. But you know that this life is what you're due, because of all your sins. And one day, a brave but frightened boy decides to climb the mountain, even though all the villagers tell him not to." Her expression darkened. "'Mount Kahna doesn't wish to be disturbed!' the villagers say. 'It will eat you alive!'" She snatched at the air in front of their faces and they all flinched, even though she'd done this dozens of times before. "And you know they're right, because the mountain only loves evil things, like you. But this boy doesn't listen to the villagers. He fills his lucky bronze canteen and sets out anyway. And this makes you happy because—"

"Wait," said Hetsbi, frowning. "You forgot the eyes."

Oh, right! Lalani realized that, too. The eyes were the most important part of the story.

Veyda tossed her long, raven hair over her shoulder and braided it, something she did when she was impatient.

"Ah, yes, the eyes," Lo Yuzi said. She sighed and leaned back. *Creak.* "I suppose we'll have to start again another time."

"Just backtrack a little bit and we can keep going," said Lalani quickly.

"I'd rather start a new path than trace old ones," Lo Yuzi said. "Besides, it's time for sleep. We need to wake as early as we can to beat the sun."

But there was no point in that, and they all knew

it. There'd been no rain for months, and the heat was relentless. It didn't matter what time you woke up, you were going to sweat.

Veyda was already half standing. Lo Yuzi snapped her fingers toward her daughter and motioned for her to sit back down. "We have benediction."

Veyda sighed and took her seat again.

Lo Yuzi bowed her head. Lalani did, too.

"Mount Kahna," they all said in unison—although Lalani suspected Veyda wasn't saying a word. "Spare us another night. Remain quiet and peaceful in our gratitude."

Once they were nestled in their oostrum-stuffed blankets, which splayed across the floor of the sleeping room, Veyda grumbled as usual about the benedictions.

"It's so silly," she whispered. She turned on her side to face Lalani. Lo Yuzi was in the basin room, rinsing the vegetables they'd picked earlier that day. "Why are we asking a mountain to remain quiet? Mountains are mountains."

"Don't say that!" said Hetsbi. Lalani didn't know

another boy who spooked as easily as Hetsbi. Maybe because he didn't have a father to show him all the ways of men. Then again, many boys didn't. Not if they were children of sailors, as the three of them were.

The life of a sailor didn't last long in Sanlagita, after all.

"Either way, it's a good story," Lalani said. "I wish my mother told stories like that."

She thought of her mother's lined face and tired eyes.

"But that's all it is. A story. This place has too many of those," said Veyda.

"Maybe you should go climb it then," Hetsbi said, elbowing her in the back. "Since it's 'just a mountain.' Take a canteen and go up tomorrow and let's see how brave you are."

"I have more important things to do," said Veyda. "I need plants for Toppi's salve."

Toppi Oragleo, the sick baby three houses down.

Lalani pushed her blanket away with her feet. Too

warm for a blanket. Too warm for anything.

"I'll help you pick them," Lalani said.

Veyda smiled mournfully. "I'm not sure I'll need much help, sola. There aren't many plants left."

"Speaking of Toppi," Hetsbi said excitedly. "His sisters said they found hair on the rocks along the southern shore. *Ziva's* hair."

"Really?" Lalani said. Veyda rolled her eyes. "How do they know it's Ziva's?"

"It was long and black and stretched between the rocks like a web!" Hetsbi said, weaving his narrow fingers together. "There's no other explanation."

"All the women in the village have long, black hair," Veyda said. "It could belong to anyone."

Hetsbi dropped his arms to his sides. "But how did it get between the rocks then?"

"Any number of ways," said Veyda. "Like I said, this place has too many stories. We need to solve real problems, like how I'm going to make medicine without any plants."

The three of them lay there, silently.

That was a real problem indeed.

"Maybe we can ask the mountain for rain," Lalani said softly.

"I'm not asking the mountain for anything," Hetsbi whispered. "What if the mountain beast hears us? What if he's listening now, with his pointed ears, and he comes and steals us in our sleep?"

"They're just stories," Veyda said.

Lalani took her friend's hand and squeezed. "I'll ask, just in case."

She closed her eyes. *Please, Kahna, give us rain.* Her imagination floated up and up the mountain, trying to picture a peaceful benefactor. Instead, she saw the beast, just as Lo Yuzi described—except now he had sharp, pointed claws. He scrambled toward her, scuttering like a tree creature, toppling treasures in his wake.

Give me your eyes, he hissed. *And you can have anything you wish for.*

House of Light

When Lalani woke up the next morning, the sun had not yet risen over the island of Sanlagita. She found Veyda sitting on the floor of the front room with an empty basket.

"Look at these plants," said Veyda. There were a few leaves in the basket's cradle, but nothing compared to the usual number. She lifted one. Brown and wilted. "I don't know if I can use this for anything, and the baby's cough is only getting worse."

Toppi. A wiggly little boy with three older sisters. The girls had names, of course, but since they were rarely seen apart they were known simply as the Oragleo sisters. And their brother, the first boy of the family, had been sick for days. Their mother was so desperate that she had asked for Veyda's help. In secrecy—no one could ever know that a twelve-year-old girl was dispensing medicine. Not even Toppi's father, Maddux, and he was a good man. But in Sanlagita, girls had to keep secrets. Especially from the village menyoro, the man who watched over them all.

"Is there anything we can do?" Lalani asked, squatting next to her.

Veyda dropped the leaf and shrugged. "We need rain. It has to come eventually, right?"

Lalani was quiet.

"You should get home soon," said Veyda, standing. "There are men already on the water."

Lalani stood, too. Reluctantly. She hated going home. Veyda's house was alive with stories and big imaginations. And although Lalani's house looked the same, as did all houses in the village—built with wooden slats from felled trees; front, sleeping, and basin rooms for daily living—the atmosphere was something else altogether. There were invisible shadows in Lalani's house and a charged air.

There were no shadows in the Yuzi house.

Only light.